9/13/20

Hi Sibel!

This is the 15th book of

T H E

I M M O R T A L

my neighbor
Jim Lawson —
He gives with
all the poop I tried
to express this morning.
You were a Love to call.
I Thank you
Nalla

THE
IMMORTAL

JAMES LAWSON

THE IMMORTAL

iUniverse books may be ordered through booksellers or by contacting:

iUniverse
1663 Liberty Drive
Bloomington, IN 47403
www.iuniverse.com
844-349-9409

ISBN: 978-1-6632-0425-7 (sc)
ISBN: 978-1-6632-0426-4 (e)

Library of Congress Control Number: 2020912970

Print information available on the last page.

iUniverse rev. date: 07/22/2020

Acknowledgement

Thanks to Kathy, my eagle-eyed proofreader, wise counselor and loving wife

1

Strictly speaking, there's no such thing as an immortal. We call *immortal* a sports figure remembered for a generation or two. Composers or artists whose works are appreciated a few centuries or so are called *the immortals*. In fiction and myth, long-lived people are commonplace – Methuselah, the lama in *Shangri-La,* vampires and of course gods, who are immortal until people stop believing in them.

One of my favorite immortal stories is the myth of Eos, the goddess of the dawn, who fell in love with a mortal, Tithonus, and petitioned Zeus to grant him eternal life. Zeus obliged but Eos had forgotten to ask for eternal youth. So Tithonus simply got older and older, a withering husk, babbling ceaselessly, until Eos had to shut him in a room. Eventually, she turned him into a cricket.

In cosmic terms, immortality doesn't exist. Species die out, planets collapse, our sun will eventually engulf our solar system (hopefully, we'll be elsewhere when that happens) and it's said that Andromeda will one day eat our Milky Way.

So the hero of our story is immortal in a very limited sense. But that doesn't make him any less fantastic than a planetary collapse.

His parents named him Seth, the third son of Adam in the Bible, who was reputed to have lived 912 years. They were unaware of an older Seth who was the Egyptian god of evil and who dismembered his brother, Osiris, leaving his sister, Isis, to reassemble the pieces. Seth Russell's family were neither Jewish nor Egyptian so the name really didn't have any great significance other than that it was one of the most popular names at the time.

The Seth they gave birth to was healthy, happy and in no way extraordinary. He was bright and quick to learn but there was no inkling of anything that could be considered abnormal.

Somewhere around his seventh birthday, Seth's mind expanded. There was no one incident, no trauma, no sudden burst of realization, just a sense of something *more*, along with his normal consciousness.

While many psychologists think that self-awareness sets in around seven, this was different. In addition to *self* awareness, this was an awareness of something outside of him. Something foggy, distant, but *there*, nonetheless.

After a few months, a kind of clarity set in. He would be playing with his friends, lost in the fog of the game when suddenly he was aware that he was a child playing a game. And that the *he* who was a child playing a game was actually an adult. He had a vague memory of playing basketball, which made no sense since his only experience with basketball was throwing a ball at a hoop in the school yard and almost always missing.

Shortly before his eighth birthday, his parents, Paige and Ian, began to notice some unusual behavior. In their TV time before bed, Seth and his little brother, Greg, could usually agree on a suitable program for both of them, something on a nature channel that usually involved large, growling animals. But lately, Seth had been switching to a Chinese language news program. Greg kept urging him to change the channel but Seth was mesmerized by the program and every time Greg took the remote to change it, Seth took it back. Eventually, their mother intervened.

"Enough," said Paige. She took the remote and turned it off. "Bed, both of you."

As they were leaving the room, she asked Seth, "Why are you watching that anyway. You can't understand it."

"I thought I could, a little," said Seth, as Paige kissed them and shooed them out of the room.

Later that evening, as Paige and Ian were sitting on the sofa, drinking wine and half-watching the news, Paige laughed at the thought of her son going through a Chinese phase. Last year it was dinosaurs.

"Is he studying China in school?" asked Ian.

"I was curious," said Paige, "so I asked Mrs. Bertram. She said he's probably the only kid who's even heard of China. They're only Third Graders."

"So he's ahead of his class."

"I suppose so. Just be prepared for next Saturday. He wants his eighth birthday party at a Chinese restaurant."

They both sat back, amused. "The boy has excellent taste," said Ian.

"If you ask me, he's a little weird."

"That, too."

In reality, Seth could understand more than a little of the Chinese news program. The words were unfamiliar but the language was not. The cadence, the tones, the pronunciation seemed like he should know them. It was only the individual words that eluded him.

S eth's *precocity*, if that's what it was, had not gone unnoticed by his Third Grade teacher, Edith Bertram. She was a large woman in her fifties, a teetotaler, unmarried and noted for her wisdom and kindness. In her thirty years teaching at St. Andrew's, she had seen virtually every kind of student and was not likely to be surprised by anything. But she was alert to any deviations from the norm and always curious about them.

In the teacher's lounge, shortly before Seth's birthday, she fell to chatting with Beatrice Stein, a thin, pinched woman of forty-five who taught Second Grade.

"How's your class this year?" Edith asked Beatrice.

It was early October and they were only a few weeks into the year so Beatrice merely shrugged. "Nobody's killed anybody yet. They're sweet children, for the most part. How's Third Grade?"

"No surprises yet," said Edith. "I'm curious – was Seth Russell in your class last year?"

"Yes."

"Notice anything unusual about him?"

Beatrice hadn't. "Nice, bright little boy."

"Intelligent?"

Beatrice shrugged. "Well, yes, but no more than most of the kids. He didn't stand out. If anything, I'd have to say he was normal. Why do you ask?"

"I'm not sure," said Edith. "He seems to be on a different wavelength than the other kids."

"ADHD?"

"No, if anything just the opposite. It's not as if he *knows* more than the other kids, it's that he *acts* as if he knows more – it's hard to explain."

"That wasn't my experience," said Beatrice. "He was just a normal, happy child. His academic skills were average."

"It's not his academic skills – he's eager to learn and works hard. But he doesn't join in the silliness. Third Graders can be awfully silly but not Seth. It's as if he's watching the other kids from a distance."

It was obvious that something had happened between Second and Third Grades. They both paused to consider this. Edith suspected some kind of trauma.

"How's my favorite, Amy?" asked Beatrice.

"She's one of the silliest."

On the way to the restaurant with his parents, his brother, a cousin and friends from his school, Chinese memories kept pressing into Seth's mind, almost overwhelming the banter of his friends. For the past few weeks, he remembered an entirely different life but few details. He had not the slightest suspicion that what he was remembering was a past life – possibly a parallel life. He had fleeting visions of cutting up vegetables in a kitchen, of a group of unnamed but familiar friends gathered around a radio listening to a basketball game, of being bigger and possibly older than he was now, perhaps in his teens, although it would be hard to quantify it. The language seemed as natural as English.

As they approached the restaurant, an aroma came to him of onions and ginger over a steamed fish that his father made – not his real father walking next to him – but another father, who was gruff and unpleasant. And he remembered the fish, steamed Wuchang, that his father and brothers made over and over again, seven days a week.

It was beginning to upset him. Who were these fathers and brothers? Where did they come from? Why was he remembering them?

"Why are you so quiet, Seth," said the father next to him.

"I'm eight years old today," he replied. "I think."

The Golden Dragon was a basic, no-frills restaurant that had been in the same location in Chinatown for over seventy years. Entering the restaurant down some steps gave one the impression of descending into the abyss.

The door opened to a dingy, ugly room without any embellishments whatsoever except for some reproductions of rather ordinary landscapes on the walls.

The prices were cheap, the food ordinary, the décor non-existent, but what made it one of the most popular restaurants in Chinatown was that it was entirely predictable, utterly inauthentic and clearly set up for non-Chinese. The only Chinese families that ate there were relatives of the owners and they had a different menu.

As they entered the restaurant, Seth heard language that he clearly understood. Two waiters were setting up a table that could accommodate the ten children and two adults. They were spacing out the place settings and Seth knew exactly what they were saying. He knew he could even speak their language.

Birthday parties were daily events at the Golden Dragon and Seth's was typical. The waiters brought out paper hats and birthday napkins and the children studied a child's birthday menu that included exotic foods like Chow Mein, Chop Suey, Sweet and Sour Pork and Beef with Broccoli.

A thin, wiry waiter of about thirty arrived with chopsticks for the table. Since Seth had been designated as the birthday boy, he unsheathed a pair next to him. "I teach you chopstick," he said, smiling.

"I know how," said Seth.

"Ah, you know how," grinned the waiter. In his experience, children who said *they know how* were generally the first to ask for a fork.

"Teach the others," said Seth.

Two waiters brought out the dishes, naming each one as they set it on the table. As they were setting out bowls of rice, Seth took a deep breath and beckoned the first waiter over to him. He said something like *qing zheng wu chang yu* in a sing-song voice that startled the waiter. The waiter looked over at Ian and Paige, who were equally startled.

"Where your son learn Chinese?"

"He didn't," said Paige. "What did he say?"

"He want famous Wuchang Fish but not in market here. You go to Hubei in China for that."

"Is that where you're from?" asked Ian.

"Both of us," he said, indicating the second waiter.

The other children accepted the situation without thinking, digging into their dishes and trying to eat with chopsticks with varying degrees of success. The adults were stupefied. What was this? Where had this come from? The waiters assumed that the white boy had learned this one phrase to impress everybody.

That changed later on in the meal when Seth overheard the waiters whispering loudly. One had just come from the kitchen with news about something that excited the second waiter. Seth went over to them and spoke to them in Chinese, not in regular Mandarin but in the regional dialect in Hubei that the waiters used, which was mostly unintelligible to Mandarin speakers.

"Did you say Xinjiang beat Guangdong?" said Seth.

The waiter answered, "How do you know Chinese?"

Seth replied, "I don't know. But I never thought Xinjiang had a chance against Guangdong."

The waiter asked, "How you hear of Chinese basketball teams – little white boy?"

"I used to root for Guangdong."

"Used to?" asked the waiter, utterly perplexed.

The party continued normally, favors were given out and parents came by to pick up their children. But Paige and Ian were still in a state of shock.

When Seth's party had left, the waiters told everyone in the kitchen about the little white boy who spoke Hubei Chinese. Nobody believed them.

When the family returned home from the party, nothing was said of Seth's strange new talent until that evening, just after Greg had been shooed off to bed and Paige had settled him in with a brief story.

When she returned, she could tell that Seth was uncomfortable, sitting cross-legged in an easy chair across from Ian. Paige sat down next to Seth and took him on her lap.

"Did you have a nice birthday?" she asked.

Seth wriggled off her lap but stayed in the same chair next to her. "You want to ask me some questions," he said.

"Well, we're curious," said Paige.

"Did you really speak to the waiters in Chinese?" asked Ian.

"Was that Chinese?"

"You don't know?"

"I spoke to them in their language," said Seth.

"Where could you have possibly learned Chinese," said Ian. "Not in school."

"No."

"Do you know any Chinese children?"

"I don't know."

It was clear that Seth was growing more and more uncomfortable with this interrogation. He had no idea how he knew the language, and who the father and brothers he was remembering were. As more and more details came up, he was fairly certain that he wasn't imagining them, that this wasn't some kind of mental trick. He saw himself vividly in a family with no mother and constant labor. He remembered when he was older than he was now, perhaps in his teens, catching a horrible fever, which could not be treated.

"You don't have to tell us if you don't want to," said Paige, soothingly.

"There's nothing to tell," said Seth. "I just seem to remember it."

"From when?" asked Ian.

"I don't know."

"Could you really understand what the waiters were talking about?"

"Yes."

"What were they talking about?"

"Basketball."

When Seth had gone to bed, Paige and Ian sat on the sofa, nursing drinks and trying to figure out what they had just experienced.

"Some kind of neurological misconnection or something ..." said Paige.

"Or something he heard as an infant."

"Chinese basketball?"

"I know, it doesn't make sense," said Ian.

They discussed what they could do about it and couldn't think of a suitable reason to consult a neurologist. "When he asks what's the problem, what do we say?" said Ian. "That our son speaks Chinese?"

"I'm not sure that's curable," said Paige.

Perhaps a psychologist would be a better route. Or start with his teacher, Mrs. Bertrand. But did they want to bring this out into the open just yet? Maybe there was a simple explanation, although they doubted it. Maybe they should keep the whole thing under wraps because once this came out, it would be out of their control. Imagine if *The Post* or *The National Inquirer* got a hold of it, not to mention Twitter.

They went to bed thinking the best thing to do was nothing.

A peculiarity like Seth's could not be hidden or ignored for long. A week after the birthday party, Paige was called into Seth's school for a parent-teacher conference.

For Paige, a parent-teacher conference was an occasion to celebrate Seth's or Greg's accomplishments, their brightness, their social and academic skills and a catalogue of virtues like perseverance, studiousness, willingness to learn, adaptability, honesty, helpfulness. She had never had a conference where they discussed a problem, a difficulty, a matter of wrong thinking, a real worry.

This was true of Paige's life in general. The daughter and granddaughter of wealthy lawyers, Paige was brought up on the Upper East Side, with a country house in Scarborough, where they belonged to the Sleepy Hollow Country Club. She was a child of privilege and looked the part – blond, scrubbed, athletic, conservative and utterly nonconfrontational. Her life ran so smoothly that it could be said to be hardly lived at all, with the exception of giving birth and an incident from before her marriage to Ian. After college she had been engaged to a Navy officer who was killed in Iraq. Normally, she would have been devastated but she was already seeing Ian at the time, had switched her allegiance, and her fiancé's death was something of a guilty relief.

As for raising Seth and Greg, she had nurses and caretakers to take off the strain and allow her love to unfold without stress. She had already experienced the ups and downs of dealing with two emerging personalities and expected some hostility when they reached teenhood, but nothing she wasn't prepared for emotionally and psychologically. What she was *not* prepared for was this conference with Edith Bertram.

"I was surprised to get your message," said Paige, as she entered the empty classroom and accepted a seat on one side of Edith's desk.

"Were you?" said Edith. "Haven't you noticed anything unusual about Seth these days?"

"Unusual? Well, now that you mention it, he does seem a bit distracted."

Edith didn't want to waste time beating around the bush. "We caught Seth gambling and teaching the other kids how to gamble."

"How very odd. That's not something he does at home."

Edith wondered if Paige was being purposefully dense, or if that was her natural state. "He said it was a game called "Fan Tan" but there was no doubt it was gambling. Seth was the "tan kun" which means "ruler of the spreading out." Clearly, he was the house."

"He didn't learn that at home," said Paige. "Is that Chinese?"

"I assume."

"Now that you mention it, he does seem to be taking an interest in things Chinese." Paige worried that she'd have to reveal the truly startling fact that Seth spoke Chinese. She and Ian had agreed to keep it quiet.

"What about *Asumal*?"

"What's that?"

"That's what we'd like to know." Edith explained that a few days ago the class was studying the countries of the world and she showed them a big map where the children could pick out various countries. Seth had spent most of the class trying to find one country that wasn't on the map.

"Asumal?" said Paige.

"That's what it sounded like."

"Doesn't ring a bell."

Seth had been sure of the name but he didn't know where it was except that it was a hot desert country. He mentioned a village called *Horafadi*. "Does that mean anything to you? We couldn't find it on the map."

Paige shook her head. That didn't sound Chinese.

"Are you sure there's nothing going on at home?" asked Edith.

"No, not at all," said Paige. "Except that he knows how to sew."

"Sew?"

"Yes, he got a tear in the knee of one of his jeans and he sewed on a patch. I asked him where he learned to do that and he said he just remembered."

"Do you sew?" asked Edith.

"Almost never," said Paige. "Well, actually never."

This was becoming stranger by the minute. A boy, much less an 8-year-old, doesn't just pick up sewing. And if his mother never sewed, how could he have remembered it? From what? From a movie?

"Oh yes, there is one other thing," said Paige. "He whispers something like *bizma* or *bizmillah* before we have dinner."

"That doesn't sound Chinese," said Edith. "More like Arabic. You say he whispers it?"

"Under his breath. Almost like saying grace."

Edith sat back and tried to take in all that she just heard. It didn't make sense, just appearing out of the blue. "Would it be okay if I discussed Seth's symptoms with Mr. Ellis, the principal?"

"*Symptoms* – is that what they are?"

"I suppose so."

"Symptoms of what?"

"Well, that's what we have to find out," said Edith.

As confusing as memories of his Chinese childhood were, they were put in perspective by new memories crowding out his Chinese ones. He remembered a life of unmitigated misery from early childhood through the remainder of her life. *Her* life, for she was female in her memories and her only virtues were obedience, subservience and fecundity. Her environment was a village in a hot, desert scrubland, far removed from towns and there was no way out. There were no telephones, no radios, no running water, no electricity, no cars, except those used by the police or army, no possible way to communicate with the outside world and no opportunity, as she was watched constantly. Occasionally, a plane flew overhead but that had nothing to do with her world.

She was powerless, in the middle of nowhere, yet there was one major difference from the equally powerless women around her. She had the perspective of someone from outside, experiencing a dreadful life. The 8-year-old Seth Russell slowly began to realize that this was a full life, as was the Chinese one. But who was Seth Russell? His Chinese name was Liu, and the one before that, Tariqah. It took a while to dawn on him that these were his past lives.

Meanwhile, in his present life, his relationship with his classmates changed. Somehow, they seemed to sense that he was older and knew more than they did. They asked him questions about school, teachers, sex, parents, sports, games and seemed to value his answers. Which meant that he was removed from them, a space had opened up between them and he could no longer have real friends. His former best friends were more like acolytes and the honest, open enjoyment of companionship was slipping away.

In truth, he didn't really know that much and usually didn't have the answers they were seeking. His mind was that of an 8-year-old with a slew of memories that hadn't coalesced into a central viewpoint. One of the few adult facts he could pull out for the benefit of his classmates was the mechanics of sex, which most of them knew about from the internet, and the fact that it was painful for the girl, which was new to them and disturbing to the girls.

Edith Bertram, his homeroom teacher, could not fail to notice his new standing with his classmates and discussed it with the principle, Frank Ellis, a kindly man who had run the elementary school for four years, having been imported from California. He was viewed by the majority of the teachers as something of a hippie, although he dressed conservatively and was clean shaven, with a relatively short haircut. Perhaps it was because he was overly blond, with a California insouciance that people enjoyed but didn't necessarily respect.

Ellis felt that there was some cognitive anomaly going on which they should look into.

"Cognitive anomaly?" asked Edith. She assumed this was California jargon for *something strange.*

"An incongruity, a deviation from the ordinary," said Ellis. "Evidently, he's picked up this information from who knows where and it's spinning around in his head."

"The shame of it is, the kids look up to him," said Edith.

Instead of interviewing Seth himself, Ellis recommended he see the school psychologist, Dr. Orenstein.

David Orenstein had been a school psychologist for twenty-five years and considered himself wise in the devious ways of children. They lied, they omitted salient details, they conveniently forgot certain facts, they wriggled out of his more uncomfortable questions and the youngest of them cried.

Crying was a technique to avoid the truth – some of the kids were very good at it.

His office was bare and cold, with not a pencil out of place. There were no pictures on his walls to distract his patients, no flowers to give his office a human touch, no patterns in his upholstery and cushions. He wanted his office to be as featureless as possible, to give his patients no way out but to look inside themselves. It almost goes without saying that he was a bachelor, with no children of his own.

Seth came to him with a story so patently ridiculous that Orenstein almost threw him out of his office. It was several weeks after Edith's conference with Paige and in that time a host of new revelations had come to Seth and a solid understanding that these were past lives.

Seth didn't think to keep his experiences secret. When he related them, Orenstein immediately went on the offensive. "So you say these memories, or whatever they are, started when you were seven."

"That's when they usually appear," said Seth.

"Usually? I don't understand."

"Then you haven't understood anything I've been telling you," said Seth. "With every new life, memories of past lives start to appear when I'm around seven or eight."

"Okay, Seth, let's cut the crap," said Orenstein. "Why are you doing this?"

"Doing what?"

"The Chinese thing. This new thing. A parent complained to the school that you were teaching your classmates about sex."

"They asked."

"And you know all about sex because you had sex in another life."

"Yes."

"You told one little girl that sex was painful. Was that your experience?"

"Not in my last life. The one before."

Orenstein was by now thoroughly exasperated. "Oh for god's sakes. Was this the mythical country you couldn't find on the map? I can't remember what you called it."

"Asumal," said Seth. "And it's not mythical. I just don't know the name in English."

"And sex was painful in Asumal?"

"They had sewn up my vagina when I was ten. My husband had to break through."

Orenstein had to admit that Seth came up with interesting examples. "So you were a woman?"

"I was the fourth wife of Sheik Abdrashid Yusuf Ahmen, leader of the Jilible."

"The what?"

"The Jilible, a subclan of the Rahanweyn …"

"That's enough," said Orenstein, disgusted by Seth's insistence on his preposterous story. When a child creates a fantasy life in this detail, there must be a reason behind it, possibly some trauma at home or school. He began to question Seth on his home life, problems with his parents, his brother, problems at school, his teachers, bullies. Seth admitted to no problems whatsoever and provided no details. His responses were evasive, to say the least.

Finally, Seth said, "You don't believe me, do you?"

"About what?"

"My past lives."

Orenstein snorted. "I may be dumb but I'm not that dumb."

Later, he reported back to Ellis and Edith. "Clearly, he's concocted this fantasy to attract attention. The question we have to answer is *why*."

"So you don't think there's anything to it," said Ellis.

"To what? Past lives?"

"Some neurological mix-up where he remembers things that happened to other people."

"You're kidding," said Orenstein, more than ever convinced that Ellis was a new breed of California hippie.

"Well, he *did* appear to speak Chinese to the waiters in the restaurant, according to his parents. An 8-year-old doesn't go about spouting Chinese out of the blue."

Orenstein sighed. *Why do I have to deal with these idiots*, he thought. "I think he arranged a little show for his parents. Maybe he pretended to go to the bathroom and set it up with the waiters instead."

Edith interrupted. "That's possible but it doesn't explain his obvious maturity, compared to his peers."

"Edith, Frank," said Orenstein, "please put it out of your minds that there's some mystical transference of identity here, or memories of past lives. If people had past lives, we'd know about it."

"Not necessarily …" said Ellis.

"Okay, I'll grant you whatever," said Orenstein. "The point is, this child needs therapy. From my interview with him, I can see a little boy starving for attention. There are medications that might be of some help as well."

"That help reduce the need for attention?" said Ellis.

"That help reduce anxiety about it. If you like, I'll talk to his parents about it."

"Let's give it a little while longer and see what happens," said Edith.

"Whatever. But it's not going to go away. He'll just make up something else. I fear he's headed for a psychotic break," said Orenstein.

Over the next few months, more lives entered into Seth's consciousness but he couldn't tell whether they were in any order or when they occurred. Aside from the Chinese life, which he knew to be recent, the new ones came with dates that only referred to themselves, as in 'the year of the fire' or 'fourteen years after the rule of Timon' or 'ten winters after the time of troubles.' He had yet to remember a civilized life that had a recognizable date. He spent some time at his computer trying to establish dates and places, without much success.

Part of the problem was who he was in the other lives. In Asumal, for example, he was essentially a slave who received no education and was removed from outside influences. In another life, he was a nomad, where the seasons were vital but the years were unimportant. Memories would pop up from various lives as brief glimpses, a sudden flash of identity as a man, woman, child, ancient, a mélange of languages, parents, spouses, siblings thrown out haphazardly. The only certainty was that he was more than an 8-year-old American boy.

He spent more and more time by himself, trying to organize his memories, writing down what he remembered, snatches of poems, songs, stories in languages that seemed to make sense when he put his mind to it. There were some poems, songs and prayers that he remembered in their entirety, as vividly as yesterday's dinner, but these were exceptions.

One of these he exhibited at a school performance night at which everyone in the elementary school was expected to take a part. Most of his class sang "Oh What a Beautiful Morning," which they'd been practicing for a month. There were piano recitals, including a very talented Second Grader who played a Bach prelude and fugue. There was a brass quintet that lost their way through part of a Mozart serenade, and an Eighth

Grader on her way to becoming a professional diva who sang "Voi Che Sapete" from "The Marriage of Figaro."

When it was Seth's turn, he gave a little explanation before his song.

Mary Mulveny, the theater teacher who was presiding over the evening, introduced Seth's performance as a special treat, a traditional folk song from Lapland.

"This kind of song is called a "yoik," Seth explained to his audience, which included his parents and his brother, Frank Ellis, David Orenstein and Edith Bertram. "It was sung by the Sami people of Sapmi, which you probably know as Lapland. Sami's don't like to be called Lapps, it's sort of a put down. Anyway, this song is in a Sami language called "Kemi," which doesn't exist anymore. Almost nobody speaks it."

Orenstein squirmed in his seat and rolled his eyes.

"It used to be spoken in the Finnish part of Sapmi. Anyway, the yoik I'm going to sing for you is an old poem by Olof Sirma about a little reindeer doe called Kulnasatz. Usually, yoiks are improvised but this one isn't."

He began to sing a strange half-chant, half-song that had the audience mystified but intrigued.

> "Kulnasatz, nirasam,
> angas Joa oudas Jordee skadhe
> nurta wata walgesz skadhe.
> Abeide Kockit laidiede,
> Fauragaidhe sadiede ...

Paige, Ian and Greg hadn't heard the song before and were pleased but puzzled. Where had this come from?

Orenstein turned to Ellis. "So now he's a Lapp."

"Evidently."

"Singing in an extinct language."

"It would appear so."

"How convenient."

"There's something haunting about it," said Ellis.

Edith was sitting next to Beatrice Stein, the Second Grade teacher. "So when did the Lapp thing start?" she asked.

"It's new," said Edith.

"You haven't been studying Lapps?"

"No, American Indians."

Ian had no idea what Seth was singing about but Paige thought it was beautiful.

"It's stupid," said Greg.

"How much longer can he keep this up?" Orenstein whispered to Ellis.

"Keep what up?"

"The pretence."

As Seth kept singing:

> Ällå momiaiat kuckan,
> kaigawarre, patså buårest
> källueiaure tuun, Mådhe påti
> millasan, kaiga wånaide
> waiedin. Ågå niråma ...

Ellis turned to Orenstein and said, "An 8-year-old making up a language like this? It's more than a pretence."

"I admit, he's clever," said Orenstein.

"He's by far the best student in the class."

"Maybe the sickest," said Orenstein. "God knows what he'll be like as a teenager."

One of the parents in attendance, a reporter for U.P.I., wrote up a feature on Seth's performance, which went out to the news services. This was to have major repercussions later in Seth's life.

The next few years, between the Third Grade and the time he was confined to an institution at the age of twelve, were a surreal balancing act. As memories of more and more lives crowded his mind, it became more and more of a chore to concentrate on the here and now. He had to compartmentalize his mind to keep the constant influx of memories from crowding out his parents, his brother, his schoolmates, his pretense of normalcy.

At first, the lives were little more than a jumble of impressions and languages. He could speak in the Sami language, for example, calling to his brothers to help him tag a reindeer. He knew exactly what he was saying, he understood what his brother said to him, but he could never have translated it into English.

The first date he could fix on, aside from his recent life in China, in the 2000's, was in Prague in 1875. He had been apprenticed to a well-known watchmaker named Bozek, although he couldn't remember his own name. He could picture the dark warren where he and the other apprentices labored over crafting components and he had a vague memory of having apprentices of his own but nothing about his life, his parents or his wife, although he was sure he was married.

The lives didn't make sense to him. They could have been in some order, present to past, but they could just as well be random. The 1875 date in Prague was wedged in between primitive lives outside of time. In school they were studying geography and he poured over the map of the world, trying to discover where he may have lived the lives in his memory. Prague (or Praha) he could find but the primitive places could have been anywhere. Asumal was probably in Africa somewhere as it was hot and barren and

Seth's life as a woman was controlled by the strict laws of Sharia. But there were lives in wildernesses that could have been anywhere.

"What are you looking for so intently?" asked Edith one day.

"Myself," said Seth.

What is myself? he wondered, late at night, when he couldn't sleep. If not the 8-year-old boy living in New York City, if not the teen cooking in Hubei or the ageless slave in Asumal, what was he? Or she? What was the entity that lived, that experienced lives?

He realized that his memories were a kind of chaos and that it was up to him to put them in some kind of order. A major problem was that his memories were partial, sometimes just flashes. He could not remember an entire life, from childhood to death. In fact, he couldn't recall a single death, although he could remember being deathly ill in the jungle, possibly from a snake bite. Remembering, he realized, required discipline. He needed time to concentrate, away from the chores, cares, duties and pleasures of his present life.

But the present life kept intruding. He had to prove to his teachers that he could master fractions, that he could name the planets, that he could understand the three branches of government. He had to endure play dates and pretend to enjoy videogames. He had to do homework, tolerate his brother and please his parents. As removed as he felt from all these pursuits, he couldn't ignore them. He had to playact his life.

He realized that he was good at pretending to be himself and he found he could convince his peers that he could be one of them. His body and physical capacities were those of a normal child his age and he could run faster than some, slower than others. Where he couldn't hide his differences was in his class work and homework. He was not an 8-year old doing 8-year old work but an adult doing 8-year-old work. His perspective was mature; he was more focused; he could concentrate better than his peers. He breezed through the work, trying to keep from his classmates how easy it was.

The one constant during this period was the hostility of Orenstein. He never missed an opportunity to belittle Seth or denigrate his lives. He actually tried to convince Ellis that Seth was dangerous, he was on the verge of a breakdown and who knows what would happen when the floodgates of Seth's psyche were let loose? He finally got his chance the following year.

Maisie Albright, an athlete in training, who seemed to have no fear of heights, falls, being upside down or airborne, tripped on a branch while running in a Fourth Grade cross country race against the Fifth Grade on Field Day in Van Cortlandt Park. She received a significant gash in her leg, which only Seth noticed at first, as he was running behind her.

Rather than continue running, he stopped to help Maisie, who was clenching her teeth in pain. Seth lifted the leg and used his handkerchief to staunch some of the blood. "It needs stitching," he said. "I'll go find a doctor."

"No, don't go," said Maisie. "I don't want to be left alone."

Seth looked around at the woods surrounding the cross-country path. "Okay, I can stitch it until we can get you to a doctor."

"You can?"

"It'll hurt."

"That's okay," said Maisie.

Scanning the woods, he saw what he was looking for, a thin vine curling around a tree. It wasn't ideal but it would do. He/she had stitched wounds dozens of times, when the warriors returned from a battle. Normally, she would have collected large ants for the stitching, using their pincers to close the wound and then breaking off the rest of the body. But sometimes they couldn't be found and she had to use vines.

He broke off a thin vine from the tree, moistened the tip with his teeth and gnawed off the end to form a primitive needle. He returned to Maisie. They both had carried a plastic bottle of water and he poured the contents of his onto the wound. Then he held one end closed. "Are you ready?" he asked.

"Do it."

He passed the tip of the vine through both layers of skin and Maisie screamed. She never expected it to hurt so much.

As bad luck would have it, Orenstein, one of whose extra-curricular activities was following the cross-country runners to catch stragglers or injured runners, happened to appear at that very moment.

"Stop," he shouted. "What are you doing with that girl?"

"Sewing up her wound," said Seth, calmly.

"Get away from her."

"Not yet," said Seth. He pushed his improvised "needle" through another layer of flesh, to another scream from Maisie.

Orenstein forcibly pulled Seth away from Maisie, without bothering to look at the gash in Maisie's leg. He took out his cell.

"Are you calling for an ambulance?" asked Seth.

"I'm calling the police," said Orenstein.

O renstein had his way. Believing that Seth had been torturing Maisie, he tried to convince Ellis, Seth's teachers and Maisie's parents that Seth was a pathological sadist, that he had taken advantage of Maisie's accident to inflict pain. No one listened to Maisie's explanation that he had been trying to help. Paige and Ian knew their son was neither pathological nor a sadist but they found it hard to believe that Seth was merely practicing what he had learned in another life. Orenstein insisted that Seth needed to be put in an institution where he could get help.

Seth agreed. He was actually grateful to Orenstein for giving him a chance to get away from school and friends and take time to get control of the lives that nearly filled his brain to overflowing. He needed the peace and solitude that an institution might afford. He was aware that therapy and activities might cut into that time, and that medications might dull his mind but he felt he could eke out more time on his own than in his normal life at home and school, with fewer distractions.

The Samuelson Clinic was a small, private psychiatric hospital for children on East 78th Street. It was an expensive option – insurance only paid for a small portion of the cost – but fortunately, Ian and Paige could afford it.

Seth had his own room, with a window overlooking tree-lined 78th Street. There were no bars on the windows and the atmosphere was relaxed, at least for him.

Despite his "torture" of Maisie, and Orenstein's accusation, Samuelson's psychiatrists did not judge Seth to be dangerous, liable to hurt others or himself, or make scenes when crossed. His only abnormality, disease almost, was his delusion that he had lived many lives. It was a benign delusion – he never presumed to know more than anyone else or insist that anyone else share his delusion.

His days weren't that different from his days outside the clinic – school, activities, time for socializing and TV – but without the press of competition or social angst. The attendants kept everything in check. There were daily therapy sessions with a psychologist, usually a Dr. Chow, and one of his parents visited every day.

The clinic wouldn't take criminally insane children, those with violent episodes, those needing constant care or so divorced from reality as to be a persistent disturbance to the other residents. There were children with "special needs," with emotional or behavioral problems, some with learning disabilities and a few who were just "neurotic," there for a rest. A few were almost completely dysfunctional.

The minute Seth saw a group of them gathered in the day room, he realized, with some relief, that he was very unlikely to make friends with any of them or be pulled into their games. He was there to deal with his own lives, not theirs.

He never tried to hide his lives but he didn't care if anyone believed him. He had nothing to prove. Besides, the lives were useful – they kept him at Samuelson.

The medication that they had him take every morning had little or no effect. The memories kept coming on, churning in his mind like butter. At night, in bed, when he was supposed to be sleeping, he began to isolate some of his lives and concentrate on drawing out more of the details of an individual life.

As Marie Stofflet, wife of an insurgent commander in the war of the Vendée against the French republicans in 1793, she remembered reports of the rebel troops crossing the Loire towards Granville, where the British ships were supposed to meet them with an army of exiles. She waited in Nantes, with their infant daughter, while reports of the Vendéen army grew terrifyingly ominous. Her heroic husband first capitulated to the republicans, then renounced his capitulation. She never heard what happened to him.

Her fate and that of Pitou, her daughter, was seared into Seth's mind. Having survived starvation and disease in Nantes, they were the victims of General Lefebvre's order to drown the rebels, almost all women and children, including five infants and a blind man, in Bourgneuf Bay, the final mass drownings of the republicans' revenge. She remembered they were herded onto barges, hoping they would be taken across the bay to some sort of exile, perhaps deported to a penal colony. They were packed together so tightly it was hard to breathe. She held Pitou as high as she could but couldn't stop her crying. When the barges were pulled to the middle of the bay, the bottom of the barges gave way.

She remembered the shock of the drop, utterly unexpected. It was January, and the freezing water was a second shock. She held on to Pitou and churned her legs to get some kind of leverage but people were pressing desperately around her, holding her down. As the water filled her nose and mouth, she struggled until the agony of asphyxiation took over and blotted out her consciousness. Her last thought was that if she let go, Pitou might float to the top. She awoke gradually, as an infant in a dry, hot desert with relatively gentle savages.

It was the middle of the night when he recalled the details of his/her fate during the French Revolution. He lay in bed sweating and gasping for breath. A night nurse, Kathleen Doherty, looked in on him and came over to his side, worried.

"Are you alright?"

"Drowning," said Seth.

She sat on the edge of the bed and took his hand. "There's no water here."

"I'm remembering a past life."

"It's just a memory," she said, having been cautioned not to contradict the patients. "You're safe here."

He wasn't allowed to have a computer in his room but the next morning he went online and discovered that his/her husband had been captured and shot a year after she had been drowned. He tried to remember: what were the issues? She had been on the side of the king and the aristocrats, the wrong side.

The rest of the day, when he could get away from classes and activities, he immersed himself in his life as a woman in 18th Century France, her childhood in Nantes, one of the main ports of France and a major center of the slave trade. In her childhood, she spoke Gallo, a regional language, and only later did she learn French.

Slowly, Seth was able to reconstruct much of her life as a girl, woman, wife and mother in Bertaeyn, the Gallo name for her home in Brittany. She remembered a little about her childhood, her meeting with Jean-Nicolas and the utter stupefaction he evoked when he asked her father for her hand. Her father had resisted, as Jean-Nicholas was the son of a miller from a family of no consequence in Lorraine but he persisted and her father eventually acquiesced.

Jean-Nicolas rose from the ranks of the royal army to become a Major General in a hopeless cause. Marie remembered the pangs of childbirth, aggravated by worry over Jean-Nicolas, who was away from home at the time and in constant danger.

By the end of the day, he found he could place the whole life in a separate compartment of his mind and simply forget about it, although he could recall any part of it at a moment's notice. By light's out, when Kathleen came by to see how he was doing, he was already asleep.

Other lives were waiting to be examined but Seth called a moratorium on introspection until he had fully integrated his life and death in Bertaeyn. He described the life in detail to his assigned therapist, Henry Chow, a mild-mannered, somewhat bemused man in his 40's, who had been at the Samuelson Clinic for 6 years and was entirely satisfied with his position. He had settled into his job, found a wife who was equally unambitious, and looked forward to remaining where he was for life, although he realized that this was unlikely – who knows how long the clinic would remain in existence before being gobbled up by a system?

Dr. Chow listened to Seth's description with interest, if not conviction, asking questions only about details. "How long did it take you to remember (he wanted to say "construct" but thought better of it) this life?" he asked.

"I knew it was there for a year but I didn't remember the details until the night before last."

Dr. Chow nodded and obviously didn't believe a word of it. Like Dr. Orenstein, he wanted to know why Seth was making up such elaborate scenarios. Was there any purpose in this exhibition? He disagreed with Orenstein that this was simply a ruse to get attention – it must be something deeper than that. But that would come out slowly – he hadn't the slightest idea what it was.

"What was it like being a woman?" Dr. Chow probed. Was it possible that Seth could have gender issues?

"Subservient," said Seth.

"What do you mean?"

"We were taught that men were our masters. St. Paul himself said that wives should submit to their husbands as to the Lord."

"Did that make you angry?" asked Dr. Chow.

"At the time, no. It makes me angry now."

This was interesting, a possible introduction into the maze of his psyche. "Why is that?"

"I don't remember that many lives yet but in every one where I've been a woman, I've been little more than a slave, although sometimes an important one."

"What about now?"

"Now I see my mother defer to my father in more subtle ways. Back in the jungle or in the desert, the man simply beat the woman to demonstrate his superiority. Now in America it's against the law, but the potential is still there."

"The potential for what?"

"The man has to show that he's stronger, more capable, less emotional, the breadwinner, the protector – there's an unspoken assumption that, if provoked, the man could dominate the woman by violence or rape."

Dr. Chow sat back. A 10-year-old boy discussing women's issues was startling to say the least. But to speak with some understanding, with an intelligence far beyond his years, was nothing short of amazing. Where had he gotten these opinions, these examples? "Do you think your mother feels this way?" he asked, finally.

"I think all of my mothers felt this to some degree, the one I have now probably the least."

"Did she ever talk about it?"

"Not to me," said Seth. "But 21st Century American women are up in arms about being belittled. A man who acts the way men were supposed to act since the beginning of civilization would probably be arrested today."

Dr. Chow nodded in agreement. His own father had been a tyrant, lording it over his family. He felt he had the right to make everybody miserable.

They kept up the conversation about the role of women for another fifteen minutes. It became clear to Dr. Chow that this boy was difficult to characterize. On the one hand, he might be a genius, intellectually and socially. On the other hand, Seth was convinced of something that was patently absurd. Was his belief in his own personal afterlives pathological?

Dr. Chow couldn't decide.

What Dr. Chow *could* decide was that Seth was clearly a genius in some respect and that his education should be accelerated. Even without testing, Dr. Chow knew that Seth was on another level from even an advanced Fourth Grader – he could even be at a high school level. Samuelson's own elementary school was not capable of handling a student like Seth. He'd have to explore other avenues.

He had the elementary school teachers put Seth through a series of tests. He passed the Fourth and Fifth Grade exams without studying. He asked for a day to study the Sixth Grade final exam. He needed to bone up on current science, contemporary history and the use of computers. Given an extra day to study, he aced the Sixth Grade exams.

The teachers at the Samuelson school agreed that Seth was now ready for Seventh Grade work, perhaps even Eighth Grade. They wondered if he could pass the admissions tests for the specialized high schools like Stuyvesant or Bronx Science, which were only open to Seventh and Eighth graders. Hunter, another school for gifted children, was only open to Seventh Graders.

Eventually, Dr. Chow and the teachers and administration at Samuelson's school decided to keep Seth in their own school, in Seventh Grade. It was easier than going through the testing, paperwork and politics of putting him in another school. As the clinic's school stopped at Eighth Grade, they'd have him tested for Stuyvesant at that time.

Whether Seth would silently submit to the plans for him was another story.

I t was no surprise when I, Tshuin, became an uwishin of the Shuar. When I was seven, just when the visions of other lives started, my father apprenticed me to a master uwishin who breathed into the crown of my head to give me health and peace and then had me drink the sacred natem, which gave me visions and spirit power. At first, it was a bit difficult to sort the shuar visions from the life memories but, after a while, both gave me power.

My mother and grandmother taught me medicinal plants and the healing chants but it was my uwishin who showed me how to use the spirits to heal, to grow crops, to find out our enemies' plans in warfare, to placate hostile spirits and predict the future. My apprenticeship was long and arduous, with much fasting and dreaming, weeks living alone by the river or under the river with a mermaid, who fed me the meat of the boa, which was poisonous to the uninitiated.

Because I was an apprentice uwishin, I didn't have to kill to take my wives like ordinary Shuars. Mine were captured in a raid on the Humabisa, where I shrank the head of their father and hung the head around my waist to contain his spirit and add it to my own. But once I was a full uwishin, I attended raids, killed an Achura uwishin with a dart and brought back a head of my own, to the delight of my wives.

They watched in rapture as I stripped the skin from the skull, sewed up the eyes and mouth and boiled the skin until it shrank to a third of its size. Then I stuffed the skin with rocks and sand and polished the head with a stone, all the while remembering my civilized life making watches in Prague and realizing that I couldn't leave my Shuar family until death.

One day, three strange looking men came to our compound, accompanied by an Aguaruna interpreter. I could sense a glint of power in the Aguaruna but none of the other men had souls, although they had killed enough to acquire them.

They gathered us around them and one of them, the one who spoke, was the strangest looking one of them of all. His skin was white and his eyes were round. His brown beard was not full but clipped, growing around his nose and chin. He wore light armor and carried a sword. From my other lives, I recognized him as European but my extended family had never seen his like and were wary of it.

The spokesman said he represented a powerful king who ruled over a vast territory and that we were part of his dominions. To show us how much he cared for us, he would give us the one true religion so that we could be saved and enter into heaven after death.

The second man, who wore a long robe and what seemed like a sacred charm around his neck, spoke to us of the danger we were in from evil-doing and savagery. He detailed the horrors of hell and showed us how to avoid them by worshipping a dead man who died on a cross.

Having lived many lives in Europe and Asia, I knew this was nonsense but I was curious to see how my family took it. I was pleased to see that everyone was skeptical. My second wife, Nunkui, named after the goddess of agriculture, thought that we should kill these people and absorb their spirits but my eldest son, Tomi, thought this would be impolite.

I was the only one aware of how dangerous these men were. In my other lives, I had seen how they burned people at the stake and used their religion as a means to enslave whole populations. But I didn't feel I could summarily dismiss them. "What else do you offer?" I asked.

"What do you mean?" asked the spokesman.

"What will you give us for adopting your religion and acknowledging your king?"

He took out his sword and a variety of daggers. The third man presented a steel-tipped lance and said that each adult member of our family would be supplied with one, knowing that our women as well as our men take part in warfare.

"Is that all?" I asked.

"What more do you want?"

"Your invisible darts," I replied. "Your magic. You must come to us in our dreams and we will discuss it there."

The man in the long robe responded. "The magic we bring you is the power of the lord god, who washes away the sins of the world."

There was no word for "sin" in our language but I knew what he meant from past lives. The others were mystified. As the interpreter translated the word into "evil-doing," what the man in the robe said made no sense. How can you wash away evil-doing that has already been committed?

The spokesman noticed the shrunken head attached to my waist and wanted to know what it was. When I explained that it was what we do to our enemies to absorb their spirit, he seemed fascinated and asked if he could buy it from me.

"Then you would have his spirit and I would not," I said.

"Savagery!" said the man in the robe.

Again, there was no fitting translation but I knew what it meant. Everyone else understood the tone of his voice and that he was demeaning us. We arose as a group and the foreigners realized that they were no longer wanted.

The spokesman rebuked the man in the robe with words that were not translated and they left quickly, leaving the lance and the daggers on the ground but taking the sword.

I explained to the group that these men were dangerous and wanted to enslave us. They considered themselves superior to us and their god superior to our gods. They would return in force and I said we should warn the other families in our area.

I don't know whether they returned or not because a few days later, I was weeding in our garden with my second daughter, Taki, when I felt a sting on my neck.

Instantly, I knew what it was. A poisoned dart had pierced my neck and that would be the end of my life. My sons would be killed, my wives and daughters taken to live with their captors.

The poison worked quickly. I had time to see an uwishin from Achura whom I knew was jealous of my skill and wanted it for himself, emerge from the jungle. The head hanging from my waist was one of his relatives. As I fell over, I saw other figures surrounding me.

The poison was curare, which all of us used, and it left me unable to move but still conscious and able to feel pain. My death would be quick if he removed my head before the skinning process but that was not to be.

I heard the uwishin describe to me what was to happen next. "I will remove your head, starting with the skin around your neck and make a cut around the back of your skull. Then I will peel the skin from your face until I have made sure I can safely remove your head from your body. Then, your face will be boiled until it has shrunk to one-third its size and I can sew up your eyes and mouth. Your head will hang from my belt with your hair and I will know what you know."

I have no idea how long the process lasted. It was indescribably painful but eventually night took over and I awoke without thoughts or memories in a cold climate.

10

The memories of his life with the Shuar did not cripple Seth in the way his memories of the war of the Vendée had, although the death was equally as horrifying. He described the life to Dr. Chow, whose first comment was, "Well, you have quite an imagination."

It seemed incredible to Seth that Dr. Chow, a trained psychologist, had simply set aside the details of his Shuar life as figments of his imagination, without bothering to check if they were true. Dr. Chow was so enamored of his own worldview that he wasn't even curious about Seth's, except as it manifested his "delusion." He sought for clues in Seth's current life that might account for these stories. He was willing to wait for years, if necessary, for clues to emerge.

Meanwhile Seth entered Seventh Grade as a 10-year-old studying with 12-year-olds, who were just exhibiting the inroads of puberty. Although Seth's small stature and physical vulnerability should have made him a target for bullying, Seth's manner was so measured and adult that his classmates, for the most part, looked up to him and asked his advice. Whether this would be true in a normal school is debatable. Samuelson was a clinic and a school for children with social and emotional problems. Whether Seth could have existed in mainstream schools just as easily remained to be seen.

It was clear to everyone at Samuelson – teachers, students, doctors, administrators, as well as Seth's parents and former teachers – that there was really nothing wrong with Seth that required a special school and a clinical environment. His only symptom was this delusion of past lives. Although he could have gone back to his old private school, or any number of schools, it was his choice to stay at Samuelson and his parents went along with it.

Even the students in his Seventh Grade class wondered why he was there. "You don't have ADHD," said Peter Bowles, a Rangers fan and video game addict. "You don't have behavior problems. You don't have emotional problems. You're smarter than any of us. So why are you here?"

"I'm an alcoholic," said Seth.

"No," said Peter, genuinely surprised.

"Not now but I was," said Seth. "I had such a bad drinking problem that my wife left me."

Peter smiled. "Oh, I get it. You're crazy."

Classes were small and everyone knew each other fairly well. Not all the children lived at the clinic and there were frequent get-togethers at private homes. Paige and Ian hosted the class for Seth's 11th birthday party.

"It's my pre-puberty party," said Seth.

"What does that mean?" asked Annie, a girl with severe dyslexia and a quirky mind.

"Well, you've all reached the age of stupidity. The guys are jerking off and the girls are getting ready for the meat market."

"What are you talking about?" asked Annie.

"Puberty," said Seth.

Although he didn't see anything interesting in Seventh Grade antics, he did make some concessions to adolescence. He learned how to skateboard and, though he couldn't keep up with his more athletic classmates, he learned a few tricks and wasn't considered totally inept by his peers. Although he was almost required to have accounts on Instagram, Twitter and Facebook, he had no real interest in sharing his opinions or listening to others. Nothing online particularly fazed him – it seemed too impersonal to merit an emotion.

He had to keep up the pretense of being a Seventh Grader while viewing that world through a prism of hundreds of years of experience. He had lived through the cusp of adolescence innumerable times in innumerable cultures but he had never experienced the freedom and lack of restraint of 21st Century American adolescents.

The music and dancing were similar to primitive tribes, where it often led to sex, then and now. The absence of religion, or ingrained superstition, was new, even in modern China where they paid lip service to atheism but worshipped their ancestors. He had met atheists in every civilized culture but they were the exceptions and very often paid for it. Here atheism had no repercussions – although this was perhaps because he lived in New York – it might be different in Texas or Mississippi, certainly in Utah.

He kept up with the news online and was not surprised to see politicians make the same mistakes over and over again, as they had for hundreds, even thousands, of years. In school they openly discussed issues that had only been whispered among friends: homosexuality, abortion, orgasms, spousal abuse, elder abuse, sexual harassment and the like. Transsexuals and gender reassignment simply didn't exist in ages past. They were free to discuss the existence of god, the possibility that other religions might contain some truth, the evils of the established church and the white WASP establishment.

In his class there were blacks, whites and orientals together, which was not possible in any of his other lives. He had been all three at various times and knew firsthand the various indignities the blacks and orientals had suffered at the hands of the whites. The other difference was the presence of women on an equal level with men. In his civilized lives, the sexes were mostly separate. In his primitive lives, women had a different role than men, and were always subject to abduction and rape. Here, in a single classroom, were militant women, militant blacks, disdainful orientals and abashed whites, who still harbored a sense of superiority, albeit squashed by convention.

In a class discussion on Thoreau, one girl described *Walden Pond* as "bullshit."

"It's not all bullshit," said another. "Maybe a little fucked up here and there."

The class laughed and Seth mused that never in any of his other lives had people, especially women, used swear words so naturally. They had lost their significance – not entirely, because people still swore in anger – but now they were part of ordinary discourse. In former times, they were the province of soldiers, peasants, serfs and the lowest levels of society, sometimes a male of the upper classes might use profanity for effect, but never around women. Profanity was forbidden for women in public. It was expressly forbidden in the Third Commandment and was considered a sign of vulgarity and low breeding, inconceivable in polite society. Yet now it was being used as part of the language.

As Seth progressed through the Seventh and Eighth Grades, there were many revelations about 21st Century life in America that astonished him.

An example was a class discussion about the use of "cruel and unusual punishment," which was officially banned in the U.S. Constitution. Although a few other countries had given lip service to similar bans, the absence of public torture and execution was a major break from accepted practice over the centuries. The Americans in his class and others he had met were absolutely shocked at the stonings practiced by ISIS, Al Quaeda, Saudi Arabia and Islamic countries from Iran to Mauritania, as permitted by Sharia laws. But in most of his lives, stoning or execution by public torture was common and legal, a public entertainment. The absence of this, and the shock of its contemporary presence, was a welcome departure from the past. Although, if truth be told, he had attended executions in many of his lives, and enjoyed some of them, for particularly heinous crimes.

The other notable break from the past was the absence of officially sanctioned slavery, except in parts of the Middle East. In most of his lives, slavery was a fact of life; it wasn't even questioned. The Bible and Koran accepted it completely. From time immemorial there had been isolated outcries against the institution but these hadn't begun to gather momentum until the late 18th and early 19th Centuries. In class, they studied the Emancipation Proclamation and its aftermath in the continuing persecution of African Americans. A hot topic was sexual slavery, practiced in almost every country up to the present day. But this was officially condemned and forces were gathered to suppress it, albeit inadequate. In most of Seth's lives, sexual slavery was openly practiced and approved of. Seth had been a slave himself, and herself, in several short, brutal lives.

Looking at his fellow classmates, Seth had to remind himself constantly that he was supposed to be one of these children, exceptionally bright but still one with no legal rights, one who would not be taken seriously by the adult world. As for adults themselves, they seemed like children as well, although he liked most of them, especially the night nurse, Kathleen Doherty, who continued to drop by Seth's bed every night to wish him well. She reminded him of a woman he had known many lives ago – he couldn't remember where, possibly in Finland.

But then, so many of the people around him seemed familiar. There were certain expressions, facial types and body carriage that transcended race or time. One boy at Samuelson, Peter, had a quizzical owl-like face, which he remembered from his second wife, Gaositwe, of the Bangwaketse, in what became Bechuanaland, and also Aloicia, her best friend in Venice around the First Crusade. Others had a sharp hawk face, or a wry simian face, types he had seen in every age, including the present. He saw less discrimination in this age and country than in the past – to discriminate on the basis of sex, race, color or religion was now frowned upon, and for the most part illegal, although still practiced of course.

Eons ago, he had experienced automatic discrimination as one of the Nommo people of Bandiagara, whom the Dogons called the Tellem. (Their name, Nommo, was given to one of the principle gods of the Dogons.) The Dogons and other large raiders chased them out of their caves and mud brick homes mostly because they were small. It was similar to the way people saw Munchkins today, dwarves, buffoons, unable to protect themselves, and to whom no respect was due. Wherever they went, they elicited a superior smile. Even as the first wife of a shaman, she knew she could never be taken seriously by the "normal" people outside. With the insight from former lives, she kept asking herself, why, *why was I given this ridiculous body.* But no one else thought it was ridiculous until the Dogons arrived. They had traded with large people before, people who smiled at them and tried to cheat them, people who thought their diminutive size was an excuse to dismiss them as fellow humans. One of them offered to buy Sigi's aunt for use as a toy. (Later on, their ancestors were displayed in zoos.) Alone among the Nommo, she felt trapped in her body, aching for release, which came only too quickly.

Her most vivid memory of her short life in the caves of Bandiagara was not her childhood, which was neither happy nor sad but just *was*, nor the laughter and endless songs in the encampments outside the caves, nor the time of troubles, when the large people infiltrated their territory, led by their evil spirits, but the manner of her death. She knew what it was from past lives, but had never experienced it, the fever and chills, the boils in her armpits and blackening of her fingers and toes. It felt like a demon had taken over her body and the torment was terrible. What was worse was the fear she inspired in her family. Her husband was brave enough to do the healing rituals in her presence but at a distance. No one would approach her. Food and water were left on the ground in front of her and occasionally a relative would peep in her cave and call out a greeting but, for the most part, she was entirely alone, dreaming of happy times in other lives. She tried to warn Ogotem, her husband and the chief shaman of her people, that she had contracted plague and that everyone was in grave danger but by that time, she couldn't speak. She passed out into another life and had no idea what happened to her people.

It took him several days to recover from a memory like this. He obsessed over details, major and minor, like the feel of Ogotem's body inside hers, or the haunting half songs/half chants that went on for hours and evoked a maelstrom of emotions, or the burial of her grandfather, Ndili, in one of the highest caves, stocked with spirit food.

There were no bars on the windows of the Samuelson Clinic. The doors were unlocked during the day. So it came as no surprise to his classmates when Seth disappeared from time to time to process a memory, like his life among the Nommo. Usually, he went to the library at 42nd Street, or sat on a bench in Central Park or down at the Battery. Nevertheless, his brief absences always came as a surprise to Dr. Chow and his teachers. Seth had seemed too *grounded* and predictable, despite his fantasies. His parents were called but they never had any idea where he was. "He goes where he goes," said one of his classmates.

By Eighth Grade, he had better control of his memories. They didn't paralyze him. He could usually fit them into a slot in his mind that could be accessed at will. He made no secret of his lives with his classmates or his doctors but he was beginning to think he should make an attempt to hide them. He knew that everyone took his reincarnations with a grain of salt or outright disbelief. Some of his classmates kidded him gently at first but by the end of Seventh Grade and beginning of Eighth Grade, he began to sense an undercurrent of hostility. He overheard two of his classmates talking about him.

"He thinks he's better than us," said one.

"Well, maybe he is," said the other.

"Maybe he isn't."

He tried not to let his lives interfere with his schoolwork but it was hard for him to suppress his amazement at what he was learning, especially in the sciences. With the exception of mathematics, almost everything he had been taught in the past had been wrong or so outdated as to be meaningless.

Even as late as the 17ᵗʰ Century, when he had lived in the Dutch Republic, one of the most enlightened nations in Europe, in the era of Newton and Leibnitz, he wasn't sure if the sun revolved around the earth or the earth revolved around the sun, if the stars were fixed or revolved around the earth. He was a cooper (a barrel maker) named Jaap, who knew nothing of science, only that astrology could predict the future, sometimes. He had heard of atoms but didn't believe in them.

In earlier centuries, he had been less ignorant. In Persia in the 15ᵗʰ Century, and earlier in Granada before the conquest by the Christian barbarians, he had been exposed to the scientific theories of the Arabian world, which were far in advance of Western Europe at the time. But he wasn't prepared for the onslaught of knowledge that was taken for granted in the Eighth Grade at Samuelson school.

Some concepts bedeviled him. The idea of a light year, for example. "I don't understand how light can travel," he asked in class. "Light is light."

The teacher was amused and started to explain about photons and electromagnetic radiation.

"You mean light actually *moves*?" asked Seth.

"Yes, at 186,282 miles a second."

This boggled his mind. But not as much as some of the other fantastic numbers in today's science. To reach the nearest galaxy at 20,000 miles an hour would take 137,000 years. There are trillions of neutrinos traveling through us at any given moment. The human brain can process operations at about 1 exaflop per second, which is 1,000 petaflops, which is 1000 times 10 quadrillion flops per second. The numbers were insane.

It was the same with chemistry, biology, geology, even on an Eighth Grade level. The existence of neutrons, electrons, quarks, antiquarks, gravitons, gluons was beyond belief.

In China, he had been exposed to cars, the radio, TV, telephones, electric lights and the like, and in his five years of schooling before his father required his presence in the restaurant, he had learned the rudiments of arithmetic up to fractions and decimals but the curriculum was mostly political – how the party would inevitably defeat the West. Never could he have dreamed of the brave new world confronting him at Samuelson.

The most astonishing of all for Seth was the phenomenon of instant communications either by phone or internet. That he could be in New York and talk to someone in Australia in real time, as if they were in the next room, that he could retrieve information about any subject in the world instantly over the internet, that he could connect with people all over the world on Facebook or Twitter, was a revelation to him. This was unique in human history.

When he thought of the time and effort it took to travel from Tabriz to Fars in the 15th Century or from Paris to Nantes in the 17th Century, or the time it took to get a message from one end of a battlefield to another, or to arrange a simple time to meet, he was clearly in a totally different eon.

He made use of it to research as many of his lives as he could. For many of them there was no information to be found, especially the primitive ones – the names he used and the places they lived had no correlation with the names on the map. But there was a wealth of information about his lives in Western Europe, the near East and Japan, some false but mostly true. Where most of his classmates spent their free time on video games, he spent his on Wikipedia and other sources, trying to recreate his past.

Life went on at Samuelson. Seth was as usual the top of his class academically. He had friends but no pals. While he made an attempt to fit in, he could not avoid the fact that he was two years younger than anybody else, smaller and weaker, and that he was clearly *different*, in an institution where everyone was considered different from *normal* children. A major difference was that everyone else was in the midst of puberty, a state that Seth as a male looked forward to and Seth as a female dreaded. His own body was still that of an 11-year-old and the hormones that tormented his classmates had not yet started flowing. Needless to say, he made no romantic attachments among his classmates, although a few girls flirted with him, which they considered *safe*.

It wasn't until the following year, when he aced the admissions test and was accepted in Stuyvesant High School, that the first down appeared on his upper lip and the first erection made its expected appearance one morning. He had decided to remain at Samuelson during his first year at high school. He wanted one more year to consolidate his memories.

It was rather lonely for him that year. His class had graduated; he had made no connections with the children his own age in lower classes. He knew some attendants and his personal psychologist, Dr. Chow. His closest friend was the night nurse, Kathleen Doherty, who still found the time to check on him every night.

Kathleen was 28 years old, of indisputably Irish background with a bright, healthy disposition. She had originally taken the night job because it gave her time away from her husband, whom she did not like at all. She divorced him the year Seth went to Stuyvesant.

Kathleen felt sorry for Seth. She viewed him as a brilliant but isolated boy who lived a fantasy that was both ridiculous and seductive. The boy certainly seemed mature and self-controlled but she felt there was an inner child mournfully unhappy and desperately seeking companionship.

She was also attracted to Seth in ways she found profoundly uncomfortable. She had always been struck by the beauty of children and guiltily enjoyed the bodies of teenage boys, not that she would ever pursue that enjoyment beyond mere admiration. She was aware when Seth displayed the first signs of puberty and amused when she sensed that Seth was attracted to her physically – she had more than once been the object of an adolescent crush.

But she did not expect to be wooed by the intelligence of a man in the body of a boy. He seemed genuinely interested in her life, her opinions, her troubles, her unfortunate marriage, her future. He was never over complimentary but just enough to make her feel important, wanted, perhaps even loved. Slowly, over the course of a year, they became more and more intimate. Eventually, she allowed him to touch her and she was astounded to find him so expert, both gentle and firm, the way she had always hoped someone would touch her, the way her husband never did.

"Close your eyes," he said one time.

As he caressed her, he sang a haunting tune that seemed to come from another time, almost another dimension.

> *"Dilam dar aashiqui aawareh shud*
> *aawareh tar baada, Tanam az*
> *bedilee beechareh shud beechareh*
> *tar baada. ..."*

"That's beautiful," said Kathleen. "What does it mean?"

> "My heart is a wanderer in love,
> May it remain so forever
> My life's been made miserable in love,
> May it grow more and more miserable."

"Did you write that?" asked Kathleen.

"No, it was written by a poet named Amir Khusrau who lived 200 years before me, at the end of the 13th Century."

"One of your many lives?"

Seth shrugged.

"You know what *almost* makes me believe you?"

"What?"

"You know how to touch a woman. You know all the right spots, the rhythms, almost as if you were a woman yourself."

"I was, many times."

She tried to ignore his references to other lives. "How many years can I get for statutory rape?" she mused.

"I think it depends on the state, and the judge."

Since Kathleen had already crossed the line, there was no reason to stop. They kept up the relationship, on and off, for as long as Seth remained at Samuelson.

The other staple in his life was his official psychologist, Dr. Chow, who had the power to send him home, keep him indefinitely, order various tortures or punishments, grant or deny him privileges or order his life in the way that he (Dr. Chow) deemed judicious.

Despite this power, their sessions were invariably bland and inconclusive, showing neither progress nor regression. Today, Seth started the session in Chinese, asking if he wanted to continue in Chinese today.

"You know I can barely speak Chinese. I understand it a little but my parents spoke English at home, except around my grandparents," Dr. Chow responded.

They took their seats and began the session in the way they always began their session. "So where were we?" asked Dr. Chow.

"You were keeping me in this hospital until I was no longer a danger to society."

"I never said that," said Dr. Chow.

"You didn't have to," said Seth. "You attributed my dangerous tendencies to a series of long-standing fantasies about past lives."

"What dangerous tendencies?" asked Dr. Chow.

"I think this may have come up fifty or sixty times. I was in Fifth Grade and one of my friends fell during a race and cut her leg. I tried to sew up her wound with thread made from a vine, something I'd done a hundred times in another life, but they thought I was torturing her and that I was dangerous."

"Who thought you were dangerous?"

"Orenstein, the school psychologist."

"Do you blame him?"

"He was predisposed to be hostile."

Dr. Chow nodded – actually, he agreed with Seth. "And what about now?"

"If my fantasies are what made me dangerous, you won't declare me fit to return to society until I give up these fantasies. But I'm not ready to just yet. I'll let you know when I am."

Dr. Chow seemed pleased with Seth's response. "It looks like you're leaving some room open to change your mind. Eventually."

"As I said, I'm not ready," said Seth.

"Why not?"

"A new one came back to me this morning. It's still a little fuzzy. When they go back six or seven hundred years, they're pretty clear but beyond that I forget a lot. I only know pieces of the language, I mix them up with other lives."

Dr. Chow had heard something like this many times before. His skepticism remained firmly in place but he was resigned to Seth's latest description of a new life. Actually, he admired Seth's capacity for imagining new details.

"I remember the weight of our robes. We were supposed to wear *Juni-Hitoe*, twelve layers of clothing, but they had to be layered harmoniously, in good taste. We spent hours arranging our robes, powdering our faces, blackening our teeth."

"Blackening your teeth?" asked Dr. Chow.

"That was the custom for ladies of good family," said Seth.

"You were a woman?"

"Yes."

"When was this?"

"I have no idea," said Seth. "I know we lived in the new capital, Heian-Kyo, but all of the details are still fuzzy – I'll have to look them up."

"Why are you telling me all this, since you think I don't believe you?"

"It doesn't matter what you think," said Seth. "Telling you helps me remember. I see a woman reading to us – we were all enthralled. The Empress was there."

Dr. Chow listened passively as Seth described some minor detail that seemed to arrive in his mind that very moment. It was all quite incredible. Finally, he interrupted: "How far back do you think you'll go?" asked Dr. Chow. "Ancient Greece, Egypt, Neanderthal days?"

"Well, that *would* be interesting, wouldn't it? I'll let you know if I remember being an ape or a fish."

"I can hardly wait."

Every session seemed to go exactly the same way. They went over the same material over and over again. Seth didn't mind, however. "I find it odd that you've never once checked to see if what I'm saying has a grain of truth. If I can really speak Chinese, or Somali …"

"That's right, your Asumal turned out to be Somalia."

"Or Sami, or Jivanan or Hawaiian …"

"What if I *did* check, Seth? What if I found out you really spoke all those languages? What if I believed you?"

An amusing prospect, thought Seth. "Well, I suppose everyone would think you were crazy."

"Exactly."

They spoke for a little longer, with no hope of reaching some sort of conclusion. "Well, I'll keep using you to refresh my memory."

"Don't mention it," joked Dr. Chow.

"Anyway, I want to thank you. This is such a luxury – to be able to talk about it and have time to let it sink in. In other lives, I had to keep quiet about it or face the consequences."

"Like what?"

"In Sweden, I was burned as a witch."

50

11

The admissions committee had vetted the applications, conducted its interviews, assessed the candidates with a view to diversity, locality, legacies, quotas, needs and credentials, and was now in the process of making their final selections for the freshman class.

Adrian Perlman, a normally enthusiastic cripple of 45, gradually getting worn down by the process, was chairing the committee. "Okay, who's next?" he asked.

Clara Swartz, a bright young woman of 60, took a folder from a stack in front of her. "Seth Russell."

The name elicited a breath of recognition among the members and the sense that this might be a tricky decision.

"Ah," said Adrian. "You've all read …"

Everyone nodded at the same time. Bess Mayweather, 36, the youngest member of the committee, echoed the general thought. "Very interesting."

Adrian opened the folder and studied it for an instant. "Well, let's see," he said. "First of all, he's only 15, so we're dealing with a genius."

"Or somebody who's just terribly precocious," said Sarah Jenkins, generally acknowledged to be the most cynical member of the committee, with a predilection for rejection.

Nigel Sachs, a young admissions officer who had recently transferred from Howard University, noted the obvious. "He hasn't officially graduated from high school."

"No, but the school is willing to give him a diploma after two years," said Adrian. "And this is Stuyvesant remember."

Angel Rodriquez, a 40-year-old physicist who was moonlighting in the admissions office while waiting for an appointment in the physics department, was rifling through his transcript. "SAT's are high but not perfect."

"Evidently, he's quite a linguist," said Nigel.

Bess was reading through the transcript. "French, Chinese, Arabic, Dutch, Swedish, several African languages, classical Urdu, classical Japanese, several aboriginal languages ..."

"Has he been tested on any of these?" asked Sarah.

"French and Chinese," said Adrian. "Although Dr. Dupont said he spoke French with an odd, very old-fashioned accent."

Bess, one of the two members who had interviewed him, recalled him fondly. "At the interview, he recited a very funny love poem to me in 15th Century Urdu. Well, it wasn't funny until he translated it."

"What was he like?" asked Angel.

"Charming, mature, you couldn't imagine him being fifteen."

"Then, there's his essay," Clara brought up.

"Very funny, very esoteric," said Bess.

"His experience learning the proper clicks in one of the click languages of Botswana," said Angel. "That was a first for me."

"Do you think he's ready for college socially?" asked Nigel.

Bess was certain. "Without question."

"Well, there *is* one question," interrupted Adrian.

Everyone in the room knew about it and nodded.

"Three years in a mental institution," Adrian read.

That silenced the room for a brief moment. They'd all read the report.

"It said he was delusional but didn't give the content of his delusions," said Angel.

"I'm not sure it's legal to divulge that kind of content," said Sarah.

"I don't know if it's legal to say he was delusional," countered Angel.

"The point is," argued Bess, "he left with a clean bill of mental health. They wanted to discharge him a year before he actually left. He told me he had gotten used to the place and wanted time to study languages."

"Is there such a thing as a clean bill of health?" asked Sarah.

Nigel answered that firmly. "If we had to decide on that basis, we'd have no students at all."

There was an amused silence. No one had anything else to bring up.

Adrian took over. "Alright, show of hands. Is there anyone who *doesn't* want to accept him?"

No hands were raised.

"Done,' said Adrian. "Clara, put him on the list."

Before they considered the next candidate, the members needed a break. But before anyone mentioned coffee or a bathroom, Bess reflected aloud: "A 15-year-old who sings love poems in classical Urdu. He's going to have an interesting experience here."

"Just your typical Harvard undergrad," said Nigel.

12

Because of his age, Seth wasn't assigned to a dorm in Harvard Yard like the other freshmen but went to live on Brattle Street with the family of Dr. Paul LaPlante, a professor in the department of Romance Languages, specifically French and Francophone Studies. His principle expertise was in 18th Century literature and he was stunned to meet someone who was so fluent in the languages of 18th Century France.

Seth had to be careful. As fast as he could, he was learning to speak modern French, especially around Dr. LaPlante. He didn't want to converse with his host exclusively in 18th Century French, which might open up a can of worms. He also wanted to converse naturally with Madelaine, the professor's wife and an assistant professor in the same department, and Marie Claire, the daughter in her last year at Cambridge Latin High School. An older daughter, Alice, was in college in California.

Although they all conversed in French at home, both Paul and Madelaine commented on his Breton accent and wondered how he had acquired it.

"That was how my first French teacher spoke," explained Seth. "I didn't realize it was an accent." He hid the fact that his native language in the 18th Century was actually Gallo but sometimes a word in Gallo crept into his conversation. At dinner one time, he asked for *formaij de biq* instead of *fromage de chevre*. Paul, who was aware of Gallo, found it interesting that this mysterious first French teacher spoke an archaic language that was not entirely extinct but rare.

It was a comfortable life, living with the LaPlantes. He had his own room on the second floor, breakfast and dinner with the family and freedom to come and go as he pleased. He frequently spent late nights or sometimes all nights at Lamont, the undergraduate library, or long hours at Widener, the largest university library in the world, and the family had ceased to worry about him.

Their daughter, Marie Claire, was two years older than Seth and intensely curious about him. The LaPlantes had taken in other students too young or too handicapped for the regular dorms but she had never experienced anyone like Seth.

"So you're our latest genius," she said, on Seth's first day with the family, after they had finished a welcoming dinner and were briefly left alone while Paul and Madelaine washed the dishes.

"I'm not a genius," said Seth.

"15-years-old and you got into Harvard …"

"It's a jinx," said Seth, conspiratorially. "By the time they reach twenty, geniuses have a melt-down and end up washing dishes for a living or begging on the streets. I'd rather be known as an idiot."

Marie Claire laughed and decided she liked him. Throughout his first year at Harvard until she left for college in California, they remained close friends but never lovers. The attraction was faint and it would have been too awkward, living with her parents.

As time went on, and classes became manageable, as coffee breaks and study groups proliferated, as people got used to him and he became more of a classmate and less of a freak, he made more and more friends. They came to admire his deep intelligence and fund of information, and especially his facility with languages.

This came in handy during his second month when he was studying at Lamont in a nook on the 3ʳᵈ Floor. It was 11:30 at night and he was alone in the nook, which could seat four, reading a translation of a Japanese Pillow Book, which he had read in the original in 1064. A friend, Clay Johnson, a rough-hewn Alabaman who played classical guitar, came into the nook, breathing hard.

"Oh, there you are," he said.

"Hi, Clay, how are you?" said Seth.

"We need you."

"Why?"

"It's a matter of life and death," said Clay. "Get your stuff."

Clay explained as they cut through Harvard Yard to the dorm.

"You know Kelo, the guy from Africa?" said Clay.

"Sure," said Seth. "Tchekelo Banweng, he's from Botswana. I've met him; I don't know him."

"You have to talk him out of killing himself," said Clay.

"What?"

"He says he can't keep up and he can't go back. It's like he's the first member of his tribe or something to go to college in America, the whole village collected money ..."

"But why me?" asked Seth.

"Well, he won't go to a shrink, he won't go to his advisor, he's semi-hysterical, he doesn't know what to do. I don't know any other students from Botswana here and we heard you speak Botswanan, or whatever they speak there."

"There are 200 languages in Botswana and I don't speak the main one," said Seth.

"What's that?"

"Setswana. But why won't he speak in English?"

"I don't know, we've tried English and it doesn't seem to work. Anyway, you speak a click language and that's what he speaks when he talks to his parents on the phone."

"There are about fifty click languages there. It's highly unlikely that I speak his."

"Do what you can," said Clay.

"And even if I can speak his language, that doesn't mean I can talk him out of killing himself."

"I realize that," said Clay.

"You're desperate," said Seth.

"Whatever."

The dorm suite was quite spacious. It had a large living room/study, with a sofa, chairs, bookshelves, a kitchen alcove, a 46" TV, three bedrooms, including one with bunk beds, and its own bathroom, which is rare for a college dorm. When Seth and Clay entered, Tchekelo was sitting on the sofa looking disconsolate. Kelo was a short, intense 19-year old, with two tribal scars on his cheeks and the foundations of a beard, which might or might not develop. Sitting with him was one of his roommates, Mary Wang, a flat-faced, squat, utterly sympathetic woman, brimming with intelligence.

Clay introduced Seth to them, although they'd met him before, and said he thought Seth might be able to help out. Mary was clearly getting nowhere.

Seth spoke directly to Kelo. "Forgive a poor zosi for interrupting you."

Kelo managed a smile.

"What's a zosi?" asked Mary.

"An animal without a hoof," said Seth. "In other words a foreigner. We're all zosi."

"Good to know," said Mary.

Seth turned to Kelo and spoke to him in Nharo, a language of Southern Botswana, where he had been a midwife in the 1850's. "Do you speak Nharo?"

Kelo answered in Jul'hoan, a language of Northern Botswana, "I understand a little."

Seth couldn't understand of word of Jul'hoan, with its plethora of clicks and tones, some voiced from the nose, some from the back of the throat, some breathed out. Nharo was simple by comparison, with only four clicks and two tones. It had become the lingua franca of Southern Botswana and Namibia. "You're from the North?" Seth said, in Nharo.

Kelo nodded.

"Your language is impossible," said Seth.

Kelo answered in halting Nharo. "I can get by in Nharo, if you speak slowly."

"Let's go back to your space," said Seth, indicating Kelo's bedroom.

Half an hour later, Seth and Clay were walking back to Lamont Library. "That was amazing," said Clay. "He was like another person. What did you say to him?"

"I agreed with him," said Seth. "I thought he should kill himself. He talked me out of it."

It took a moment for that to sink in. "That's it?" said Clay.

"No, not entirely," said Seth. "He was raised a Christian but there's a god in the old religion named Kaggen who often tricks people into doing things they shouldn't. I thought it was probably that."

"How do you know about these things?" asked Clay.

"I read a lot."

"What about Kelo not keeping up with the work, flunking out and going back to his country in disgrace? I hear everyone in his village chipped in to send him here."

"Once he understood that he'd been tricked by a god, everything became understandable. There's some study counsel center that can help him free of charge, give him tutoring, whatever he needs. He's bright. He'll pass."

"Ever think of going into psychology?" said Clay.

"I thought I might be a witch doctor."

Professor Frederick Copley Olmsted was a "University Professor," considered the highest rung on the Harvard academic ladder, reserved only for the most distinguished scholars and beyond the petty confines of departments and specialties. Now in his seventies and a direct descendent of the famous landscape architect, he had the reputation of being both wise and sharp, with little patience for mediocrity in any form.

When Seth entered his office, Olmsted beckoned to him without looking up from the paper he was reading. Seth had the impression it was a studied rudeness, reserved for students and other underlings. "I'm Seth Russell, sir," he said.

"I know. Take a seat."

Seth sat on a chair in front of Dr. Olmsted's desk while the professor finished what he was reading. Officially, Dr. Olmsted was the professor of his European history class, although the class was generally taught by teaching assistants (or TA's). Seth had never actually seen Dr. Olmsted before, although he had read some of his books.

"You wanted to see me?"

"Yes."

"Is something wrong?"

"Yes."

Olmsted removed two papers from a folder on his desk. "I've read two of your papers."

"I thought the TA's did that," said Seth.

"They do, but they passed these on to me."

He held up one of Seth's papers, a 20-page essay on Venice during the crusades, which he remembered vividly as the wife of one of the laborers in the Arsenal, the principle shipyard of the Republic. "Impressive scholarship," said Olmsted.

"Thank you."

"You've made 13th-Century Venice come alive. You seem to have captured the spirit of the times, the odors, the street life, quirks of the language, details about the Venetian navy and war with the Turks. Your paper is carefully researched, your footnotes are all in order, your references show a knowledge of medieval Italian, German, Latin, French – in all a bravura job."

"I'm good with details," said Seth, modestly.

"Clearly," said Olmsted. "Since I'm not an expert on 13th Century Venice, I can't vouch for the veracity of every detail or every reference." He held out another paper. "But your second paper, on the Jews in 15th Century Grenada under the Moors *is* my field of expertise, as you know."

Seth was expecting this. He had written the paper almost from memory, having been a physician to the court of the Emir. This was one of the few lives where he'd been a man of some importance in the civilized world. He had a wife, seven children and a Moorish mistress, who bore him two other children. Although the details he included in the paper were vivid recollections, he was careful to include scholarly references to back up his memories. "I've quoted two of your books," said Seth.

"I saw that," said Olmsted, stroking his chin. As he spoke, his fingers moved from his chin to his bushy gray mustache. "I know all your references, even the obscure ones in medieval Hebrew and Arabic, Latin and Greek, not to mention medieval Spanish and French. You show an exhaustive knowledge of the times, the political issues, even the contents of a physician's carrying case.

"I got that from Dias-Mas …"

"I know where you got it, Mr. Russell," Olmsted interrupted. "I checked and double checked all your references."

"Are they incorrect?" asked Seth. "Or insufficient?"

"They don't account for all the details," said Olmsted. "As it is, I'm faced with something I can't explain, something with implications so vast that it scares me to think of them."

"I know," said Seth. The atmosphere had suddenly become charged.

Olmsted stared at Seth for a moment, then suddenly, with a slight shake, dragged himself back to reality.

"For example, on page 5 of your paper, you said that in AH 745, the Grand Rabbi of Grenada prohibited the use of wormwood on theological grounds, so the Jewish doctors of Grenada ground it to a powder, adulterated it with rose petals and called it by its Arabic name …"

"Actually, they had Moorish servants do the pulverizing."

"How can you have possibly known about this?" said Olmsted, with an expression of utter bafflement. "It's not in the literature, it's not in any of your references."

"That one may have slipped by me," said Seth.

"Or the brand of kohl that women used on their eyes, sold by an Armenian named Vardapet near the Lujayn market. Did you make that up?"

"I must have read it somewhere."

"Or the secret lottery, the abortion performed on Mulay Hassan's niece, a codicil to the pact with Castile, a new addendum to the Jewish pharmacopeia …"

"Yes, I made them up," said Seth.

"How old are you?"

"Fifteen, sir."

"You didn't make these up," said Olmsted, staring directly at Seth. "You'd need a lifetime of study to make up this kind of detail."

"So what are you suggesting?"

"Normally, I would have said you had plagiarized the whole paper, except that I can't imagine where you could have plagiarized it *from.*"

"I may be a master plagiarist."

Olmsted bristled. "Don't toy with me, Mr. Russell. I know, or know *of*, every source there is on this subject."

"That's not possible, Dr. Olmsted," said Seth. "You couldn't have gone through *all* the manuscripts at Grenada and Cordoba, or the great libraries at Chinguetti in Mauritania, or …"

"Nor *you*, Mr. Russell."

At last, Seth dropped the pretense of being a 15-year-old genius and now spoke with the presence of an ancient. "So if I didn't make up the details, or plagiarize, what is the explanation?"

Olmsted seemed too stunned to speak for a moment. He stared at Seth in disbelief but couldn't avoid his own conclusion. "You were *there*."

13

Finally, after centuries, Seth had found someone who actually believed him. In other lives, he had either kept quiet, or confided in someone who took his revelation as a joke, a metaphor, a tall tale, or evidence of insanity or witchcraft. Even if some people were inclined to believe it, they took his explanation with a grain of salt. Nobody fully accepted it.

But now there was someone. And not just a crackpot lover, or someone liable to believe anything of anyone, but a major figure in one of the most prestigious schools in the world.

Once the revelation of his past lives had been revealed and accepted, Seth and Dr. Olmsted went for a walk along the Charles River and ended up sitting on a bench, watching the sculls row past.

"How far back do you remember?" asked Olmsted, genuinely in awe of Seth.

"It's hard to keep track of time because so many of my lives used different calendars," said Seth. "When I was part of the Shuar tribe, we lived in a forest that we called "The World," and I remember our calendar was ten months long because ten was the highest number we could count. Even today, I have no idea where I was, probably someplace in the Amazon. We had no connection with the outside. But the life before that was in France at the time of the Revolution. No, wait, I was on an island before that. It's hard to keep track."

"Well, you were definitely in Granada before the Spanish took over," said Olmsted.

"Those dates I know," said Seth. "I was back in civilization. I observed Jewish dates, Hijri or Moslem dates and later on Christian dates. 1444 in the Christian calendar was the last date I remember. I assume the year I died."

"You should write this down, for your own sake," said Olmsted.

"I can't believe I'm actually talking to someone who doesn't think I'm crazy."

"The details in your papers left no room for disbelief."

"That's why I wrote them," said Seth. "So you, or someone, would believe. I've had to keep this bottled up or face the consequences, locked up as a lunatic, burned as a witch or a heretic, shunned by my parents or my people. Although there was one life where I was considered sacred. I lived in a vast desert and I remember kangaroos so it must have been Australia."

"Is what you'll be in the next life completely random?"

"If it isn't, I haven't seen the pattern yet. It seems to have no relation to what I did in a previous life. It's not karma. I'm neither punished or rewarded, just changed. Although I've begun to think the whole thing might be a punishment."

"Why?"

"It's overwhelming. And when I'm in a civilized society, I dread being sent back to some wilderness. Or being crippled, or having my clit cut off."

"You were a woman?"

"Many times. I was even a temple prostitute once. I died of alcoholism."

"So nothing you do makes any difference."

"No, that's not true," said Seth. "I learn more each time. And this life is the best of all because I can place myself in the world. I have access to the library and the internet and I can begin to see where I was, and when, in between civilized lives. For example, the country that I just knew as Asumal turned out to be Somalia. I could look up and see where I lived; I could even trace my clan. It's been a revelation, but also my worst fear."

"How so?"

"Being a woman was bad enough – even in civilized countries you were a second class citizen – but to be a woman in Somalia was unadulterated degradation. As the fourth wife of a minor sheik in the backwater of a backward country, I was basically a mutilated vagina. I had no rights, no privileges, no pleasure, no culture and no way to escape or communicate with the outside. I was stuck."

Olmsted was clearly impressed and really didn't know what to say. "How many lives to you think you've had?"

"There are too many to remember," said Seth. "I've lost most of the really early ones – I know I was alive at some time in Egypt but I don't remember any details."

"What about the great events? Did you see Christ or Buddha?"

"No, the only major events I remember were the Cultural Revolution in China, the French Revolution, the Crusades, a battle against Marcus Antonius in Egypt. I never saw anyone who's considered important now, except for Sei Shonagon and Murasaki Shikibu at the court of the Empress of Japan. I forget their real names – it wasn't polite to call people by their names."

"That would be in the 11th Century," said Olmsted.

"Yes, and I speak the court dialect of 11st Century Japanese women, which makes it hard to communicate with 21st Century Japanese. I have a lot of brushing up to do in every language."

"God, what a resource you'd be to every historian in the world, every linguist …"

"Who'd believe me?" said Seth. "Where are the references?"

"But you could provide valuable clues to help scholars."

"I intend to, but I have to be careful. I was committed to a mental hospital in this life and only got out because I denied everything. I can't be useful if I'm locked away from libraries and the internet, or too drugged to care."

Olmsted stood up and confronted Seth. "Mr. Russell, you possess the secret of life after death, the secret every human who ever lived has longed for, and fantasized about, and created religions around, and ordered their lives in the hope that they guessed right."

"I don't possess any secret at all," said Seth. "I just get blown by the wind."

"But you experience life after death, you return from the dead, something nobody else in history has ever accomplished. The very fact of it gives people hope."

"So you think I have a moral imperative to tell people, to brave the possibility of being thrown in a nut house and drugged senseless."

"What do you think?" said Olmsted.

"It's not something you can announce to the public. That's what crazy people do. By and large, if you claim to have the truth, you don't have it."

"So?"

Seth shrugged. He stood up and continued walking along the Charles with Olmsted. He knew he was supposed to have some sort of wisdom, based on over a thousand years of experience. And perhaps he did, though he didn't feel particularly wise. "Dr. Olmsted, so far you are the only person who believes me. You may or may not tell others. I didn't hide who I was when I was younger so it's possible the word will get out. Meanwhile, I suppose I could help historians and linguists, even if they don't believe me."

"Will that be your life's work?" asked Olmsted.

"My life's work is to find somebody like me."

14

Encouraged by Professor Olmsted, Seth set out to learn more about current notions of reincarnation, whether anyone else had returned from the dead – not just from a coma with dreams of immortality – but from a full life, or series of lives, as he had. Was there someone like him out there?

The obvious place to look was at the people who claimed to know about reincarnation, like Hindus and Buddhists. Seth found a likely candidate in the basement of a church in the Back Bay area of Boston. The lecture was given before a standing-room-only audience by the Asia Society of Boston. The speaker was an elderly Indian, Swami Ramavacharya, who was pretty much central casting for a swami, long white hair, a full beard, suitable wrinkles, dressed in a long white robe. He was seated on a dais and delivered a long lecture, which Seth characterized as mumbo jumbo, with references to numerous gods and ancient lore. When he was done, having answered a few respectful questions from the audience, the moderator, Professor Daikin, a sallow-looking man in his 40's, addressed the audience.

"The Asia Society would like to thank Swami Ramavacharya for his fascinating insights into the laws of karma, as set out in the Upanishads."

The Swami smiled benevolently.

"We'd also like to thank him for what seems to me his comprehensive answers to your questions. Now, if there are no other questions …"

"Excuse me," Seth called out from the back of the room.

"I'm sorry, I didn't see you back there," said Daikin. "Do you have a question for the Swami?"

"I have two questions," said Seth. "I understand that the law of karma rewards your good deeds and punishes your bad deeds in the next life. But what or who determines the specifics, what or where you'll be? Who makes the decision that I'll be a dog in Africa or a billionaire in Argentina? Is it completely random?"

Ramavacharya nodded and smiled. "Nothing is random," he said. "Some say it is Ishvara, the supreme cosmic spirit, who decides. Some say Ishvara is one manifestation of Brahma, or of Vishnu. Of the six systems of Hindu philosophy, most believe in a personal deity who assigns your place in the next life."

"So Ishvara judges the dead, like Thoth in ancient Egypt, or Christ on the day of judgment," said Seth.

"It is your deeds that determine your next life," said Ramavacharya. "The god merely executes the effects of your deeds."

Seth didn't mention how unsatisfactory this answer was but went on to his next question. "Wouldn't it help if we could remember our past lives? Why can't we?"

Ramevacharya answered almost automatically – he'd been over this material hundreds of times before. "The Scriptures are unclear on this point. Some say that memory is a physical part of the mind and the mind is recreated anew with each life. Some say the memory is exhausted in another plane between births. There are often some residual memories, or paths of thought which carry over from one life to the next."

"Do you *personally* have any of these residual memories?" Seth interrupted.

"I admit I do not," said Ramavacharya. "To remember your past lives is a discipline that requires a special kind of meditation. There are many people in India who practice this meditation, based on the sutras of Patanjali."

"Do you know any of these people?"

Ramavacharya nodded. "I've seen them in temples, in retreats, in mountain caves."

"But do you actually know anyone personally who remembers a past life?"

Professor Daikin responded to the obvious hostility of the question. "I think the cycle of birth and rebirth has been established for centuries," he said.

Seth brushed away the answer. "The cycle of birth and rebirth cannot really be established until someone remembers their past lives. Any more than Heaven can be established until somebody returns to tell us what it's like. All we have are scriptures from people who can't remember being reborn or being in Heaven."

Ramavacharya smiled. "I think we have a skeptic among us. That's as it should be."

Professor Daikin interrupted to diffuse what could be a tricky situation. "I think if most people could remember their past lives, they'd go crazy. It's something you have to prepare for. Any other questions?"

Seth left the basement with the firm conviction that Ramavacharya didn't know what he was talking about and Daikin knew even less.

15

S eth read all he could about reincarnation, mostly from Hindu and Buddhist texts, several books of the dead, including the Tibetan and Egyptian, the beliefs of ancient Greece and some Christians, and some of the religions of native Americans and Australian aborigines, some of which he had known in other lives. Little of what he read coincided with his own experience.

He read accounts of people who had claimed to remember past lives but always found them lacking, usually ridiculous. Most of the accounts were in the huge archive of pseudo-mystical literature, New Age stories, regression under hypnosis, "after-death" experiences and the like.

Just to be on the safe side, and for his own amusement, he decided to conduct a minor experiment. He placed an online ad calling for people who remembered their past lives to tell their stories as part of a Harvard project.

The ad offered no financial inducement, merely a forum for people in the Boston area to tell their stories. To make it more official, he used Professor Olmsted's influence to reserve a small classroom for the day.

He had no idea if the ad would pull at all, if anyone would respond to it. He wasn't prepared for the outpouring of responses that the ad generated in a single day. He scheduled 5-minute sessions throughout two days, with an hour for lunch and a cutoff at seven in the evening. He had a fellow student videotape the sessions and prepared himself for an interesting couple of days, with only a slim chance of finding someone like him. Still, better a slim chance than none at all.

The first respondent was a dyed-blond, bespangled woman in her 50's who claimed she was a young Confederate soldier during the Civil War. She filled out a brief form and then recounted her war experience.

"I remember floating above the battlefield at Antietam and coming down into the body of a young soldier from Tennessee. I woke up just in time to see Robert E. Lee pass by on a white horse."

"Then what?" asked Seth.

"Then I passed out."

Seth waited for more details but the woman just sat at the desk musing. "That's it?" asked Seth.

"I think he looked in my direction and felt sadness that a boy so young had given the supreme sacrifice in defense of his country."

Seth nodded and thanked the woman. A snippet from what might have been a past life but probably wasn't, or a scene from a movie or a random imagining wasn't exactly what he was looking for. He went on to the next respondent.

An obese man in his 40's claimed to be the executioner who cut off the head of "that Spanish whore." He seemed angry.

"What Spanish whore," asked Seth.

"Queen Katherine of Aragon."

"Henry the Eighth's first wife?"

"That's right."

"Queen Katherine died of cancer," said Seth.

"Oh well, the other Katherine."

No point continuing the session. Next was a man in his 60's who remembered being a field hand in Mississippi. "They called me Rastus and worked me day and night, whupped me when I was too sick to work. I remember it like it was yesterday."

"You said they called you Rastus," said Seth. "What was your real name?"

"Shaka," said the man. "I was a king in my country before the white man came over with their slave ships."

"Shaka, the king of the Zulus?" asked Seth.

The man nodded seriously.

"Shaka, who created the Zulu nation and fought the British?"

"The very same," said the man.

"Shaka, who was killed in 1828, in Africa?"

"That's the one," said the man.

"Well, thank you," said Seth.

After a few more obvious fakes, Seth was inclined to write off the experiment as a waste of time. On the other hand, he had a lineup of people coming in, so he couldn't back out now. The next respondent was a large, dreamy woman in her 30's who said she learned about her past lives through hypnotism.

"I hear that works," said Seth.

"I didn't believe it at first," said the woman. "But then, in the course of therapy, Dr. Melton had me regress farther and farther back until I was suddenly a little girl on an English lawn, in the 1800's."

"Like Alice in Wonderland," suggested Seth.

"Yes, but I didn't fall down a rabbit hole. I remember it was the day of my sister's wedding. She was marrying a man I didn't like, the Earl of something."

"Do you remember just that scene from your past life, or your whole life?"

"Just that scene," said the woman. "But I remember scenes from other lives. Dr. Melton had me regress back to Renaissance Italy."

Seth had the sense that this Dr. Melton was making a lot of money off this woman. "Was it Dr. Melton who suggested Renaissance Italy?"

"I don't remember. Perhaps. Does that mean I was making all this up?"

Seth thought this was probable but he had a few minutes before the next person was scheduled, so he asked if the memories were still vivid. She said they were. She died as a child in the English life but couldn't remember the Italian one. Seth felt sorry for the woman, who believed what this Dr. Melton told her. He didn't really want to ask the obvious question but felt it was necessary. "Do you remember any Italian?"

"The language?"

"Yes."

"Not a word," said the woman.

"Victorian England and Renaissance Italy are hundreds of years apart. Do you remember anything in between?"

"No," said the woman. "Do you think this is all untrue?"

"Hypnotized people are very suggestible," said Seth. "Your Dr. Melton may have genuinely believed he had regressed you into a past life and you went along with it."

"So you think there's no such thing as past lives?"

"I'm not saying that," said Seth. "You may have had a flash of one but there's no way of verifying it."

The woman visibly shrank with disappointment. "I want to believe it," she said, "but then I want to believe in angels."

Next was a man named Ambrose who said he was there at the crucifixion of Christ, followed by a man who was clearly medicated, who said he *was* Christ. Later on in the day, another Christ appeared.

"Do you speak Aramaic?" asked Seth to the first Christ.

"What's that?" answered the man.

The last respondent of the day, before Seth called a halt to the whole project, was an angry black woman named Latisha who said, "I got lots of past memories but I don't do it free."

"What do you charge?"

"The first three lives, $10 each," said Latisha. "The farther back you go, the more they cost."

"So Ancient Egypt, for example?"

"$100," said Latisha. "But I can tell you stuff nobody knows about, not even the professors at your school."

"Old kingdom? New kingdom?"

"Old, baby."

"That would be, say, 2500 B.C.?"

"We didn't have dates like that then," said Latisha.

Seth had only the faintest memory of ancient Egypt and he didn't know Egyptian dates but he knew some of the pharaohs from reading about them in this life. "Who was the pharaoh when you lived there? Hetepsekhemwy? Nynetjer?"

"You're going to have to cough up some dough before I answer those."

Seth had to smile at her audacity. She clearly considered the investigation as a money making proposition. She was also clearly a phony but it was the end of the day and Seth was tired. "Let's try something easier. Does my name, Seth, have any meaning for you?"

"Of course," said Latisha. "Seth was the god of chaos, the god of evil, who murdered his brother and cut him up into little pieces. How did your parents ever come up with that name?"

"They thought it was Hebrew, the third son of Adam and Eve."

"The founder of mankind," said Latisha. "I can tell you a lot about *him*, too."

Seth laughed. "Since that was so much earlier, I assume it'll cost more."

"You know it."

Seth didn't have much money on him but he was curious what Latisha had to say. "Why don't we start with a $10 life?" He reached in his back pocket, took out a $10 bill and handed it to Latisha. "Your last," he said.

She examined the bill, to make sure it wasn't counterfeit, and put it in her purse. She closed her eyes, as if conjuring up a scene in the distant past. "My last?" she said in a semi-mystical voice. "That would be in England. I was white then, a little girl with long blond hair, on an English lawn in the 1800's."

"Like Alice in Wonderland," said Seth, all hope dashed.

"Exactly," said Latisha, emphatically, "Though I didn't fall down no rabbit hole."

16

"It's been depressing," said Seth. They were in a messy office in Professor Olmsted's house on Craigie Street, not far from Longfellow's home and Harvard Square.

"I didn't think it would work," said Olmsted.

"*I* would have answered an ad like mine."

"I don't think there are too many people like you," said Olmsted.

"If I exist, there must be others."

"Why?"

Seth sighed. "I don't know. I just don't think I can bear the loneliness."

"You've borne it all these centuries, through all your past lives."

"Yes, but then I didn't have the means to search for others. I could resign myself to being unique. Now I can't."

Olmsted returned Seth's sigh. "No, I suppose not."

Olmsted had been studying a printout of an elaborate Arabic manuscript, which he had unrolled on his desk. "Perhaps you could help me with this."

He indicated two letters at the end of some sections. "The letters, "ra'a" and "da'al." They're not attached to the sentences before and after."

Seth looked at it for a moment and knew exactly what it was. "It stands for "Rex Dixit."

"But that's Latin. The manuscript is in Arabic."

"Exactly," said Seth. "When this group of scholars inserted the Latin for 'The King Says,' it stood for the Christian King or the Christian God, which meant it wasn't to be trusted. The writer put "RD" at the end of a section where he doubted the veracity of the argument."

"But that changes everything," said Olmsted, excited.

"Exactly," said Seth, dejectedly.

As he left Dr. Olmsted's house, it had started to snow. He turned up his collar, put his hands in his pockets and headed along Craigie Street towards Brattle Street. As he walked, a black limousine pulled up beside him.

"Mr. Russell?" said a voice from the backseat of the car.

Seth didn't recognize the voice and was immediately suspicious, as the limousine kept pace with his pace and seemed determined to intercept him. Instantly, he ducked in a little alleyway between houses, too small for the car to follow him.

"We just want to talk," said a voice from the car, which indicated to Seth that they wanted more.

The limousine kept moving slowly and no one left the car to follow him.

What was that about? he wondered.

He was due at a party, his first since arriving at Harvard. In his current incarnation, he would be at least four years younger than anybody there, under the age to drink, jailbait to anyone who attempted sexual relations and a minor curiosity.

The party was at a ramshackle, rather disreputable-looking house that was frequently rented by students who didn't want to live in one of the residential houses, although they were required to be affiliated with one. It had the well-deserved reputation of being a party house, as well as a refuge from the Harvard world. Naturally, it attracted a group of self-proclaimed misfits and chronic independents. There were some students who actually rented apartments in the house, and a group who just seemed to be there all the time.

One might have expected a party in this house to be something out of *Animal House*, drunken frat boys and sisters reveling in a fog of marijuana and one wouldn't be entirely wrong. There was no sense of Harvard exclusivity in this gathering but the kind of dancing, talking and necking you'd expect anywhere, with a small proportion of students who were high, drunk, sick or clearly on the make. Seth recognized quite a few of the students immediately, including a group of Chinese students who called to him as he entered. He spoke to them in Chinese until his friend, Clay Johnson, took him away to introduce him to a group of girls.

"This is my friend, Seth," he said to the group.

"Is this the famous Seth Russell?" asked one of the women, who was slightly tipsy.

"We've heard all about you," said another.

"You speak twenty languages," said a third, admiringly, to a shrug from Seth.

"Are you really only fifteen?" asked the first.

With effort, Seth managed to extricate himself from the group and eventually found himself sharing a sofa with Clay, Kelo, who had managed to stay at Harvard without killing himself, and Mary Wang, who felt she should attend a party or two just for the experience. As they chatted over a beer for Clay and ginger ales for the others, Seth couldn't help looking at a pale, serious looking girl on the far side of the room, talking with an equally serious boy.

"Who are you looking at?" asked Kelo.

"That girl over there," said Seth. "Who is she?"

Kelo and Clay shrugged. "I have no idea," said Clay. "Do you want her?"

"She's in my psyche class," said Mary. "Her name is Marike something."

"Foreign student?"

"I don't think so," said Mary. "Why?"

Seth kept staring at her; he couldn't take his eyes off of her. "She looks exactly like someone I knew a long time ago."

"Like last year?" said Mary.

"At least four centuries ago," said Seth, jokingly.

"You want me to introduce you?" asked Mary.

"It's sort of embarrassing, but yes."

Seth's excitement rose as he and Mary made their way through the party.

He recognized Marike immediately as a woman almost identical with his wife, Carinja, whom he married in 1650, and who left him a few years later after he had returned from the first war with England, crippled and bitter.

What was striking was that not only did Carinja and Marike share the same facial features, the same large brown eyes and dark blond hair, the same flushed lips and fresh, baby's skin, but the same expression, ironic, amused, somewhat cynical, brimming with intelligence but not warmth.

When they reached her, she was still in deep conversation with a very intense young man whom Mary recognized as an unpleasant predator in her Freshman dorm. Seth and Mary stood in front of them until there was a break in Marika's conversation and she couldn't help noticing the two in front of her.

"Yes?" said Marike.

"I'm Mary Wang; you're in my psyche class."

"I know."

"And this is Seth Russell. He wanted to talk to you."

Marike seemed amused by this; her companion seemed nonplussed and somewhat irritated. She smiled at Seth and introduced herself. "Hi, I'm Marike Biekman."

"Hi."

"I've heard of you," said Marike, with what seemed like an ironic smile.

"What have you heard?" asked Seth.

"Not much. Just that you're supposed to be smart for your age. You're a little young to be at Harvard but not the youngest by any means. Why do you want to talk to me?"

"Want something to drink?" said her companion. Getting no response, he left, presumably to get something for himself.

"This is going to sound strange," said Seth. "But is your background Dutch, by any chance?"

"Yes, it is."

"From far back?"

"We're one of the old Dutch families from New York. My ancestors arrived in the 1600's. This is interesting – why do you want to know this?"

"A minute," said Seth. "Do you know anything about your ancestors?"

"A little," said Marike. "The first Biekman was a cooper."

"He made barrels."

"Yes. Not many people know that."

Seth shrugged at the compliment. "It was a highly regarded profession in those days. Do you know whom he married?"

"Not really," said Marike. "The rumor is that she was an indentured servant but we don't like to admit to that."

"From Zwolle in Overijssel?"

"I have no idea," Marike brightly. "This is very mysterious."

"It may be nothing," said Seth. "pure coincidence."

"What?"

Mary had been enjoying the conversation, wondering where it would lead. "Don't stop now," she said to Seth.

"A woman named Carinja lived in Zwolle in the early to mid-1600's. She married a man named Jaap Pieterszoom, who became crippled in the wars with England and ended up an alcoholic, begging on the streets. Carinja left him and indentured herself to pay her passage to New Amsterdam."

"What does this have to do with me?" asked Marike.

Seth hesitated, as if he was about to broach a delicate subject. "There is a painting of Carinja in a private collection in Zwolle. Evidently she modeled for an artist whose name I can't remember. It was before she married Jaap."

"And?"

"It's *you*," said Seth.

"It looked like me?"

"No, it's *you*," said Seth. "There are no differences, except your hair style. The same eyes. the same eyebrows, the same skin, the same facial expressions, the same set of your mouth. Somehow the genes of Carinja got transmitted to you without any changes whatsoever."

Mary interrupted. "What did you mean when you said you knew her a long time ago?"

"Well, not literally, of course," said Seth. "Jaap Peiterszoom was my ancestor. Your ancestor may have been married to my ancestor."

"Hold up, let me take this all in," said Marike. "Did Carinja have any children by Jaap?"

"No. Jaap was my ancestor's uncle."

"So all her children, and all my ancestors, came from her marriage to Biekman in New Amsterdam."

"True," said Seth. "But she never divorced Jaap so technically all her children came out of an adulterous union with Biekman and are all illegitimate."

Marike was both stunned and amused. "Well, I've never felt particularly legitimate anyway. But where is this picture? I have to see it."

Seth grimaced. "It was in some house that tourists are supposed to see. I wouldn't even know where to find it."

"So there's no way we can tell if you're telling the truth or just making this all up," said Marike.

"Why would I do that?" asked Seth.

"To meet Marike," said Mary.

"Well, that's a good reason," said Seth. "But I didn't make it up."

Her friend returned with two beers. "Wanna beer?" he asked.

"I think I'll switch to heroin," said Marike.

Later, they left the party together and walked along Massachusetts Avenue. "Well, it's been an interesting evening," said Marike.

"For me, too," said Seth. "I never thought I'd meet a relative from the 1600's."

"I never thought I'd leave a party with a 15-year-old."

As they walked along, Seth found himself more and more attracted to Marike, much more than his attraction to Carinja four hundred years ago.

At the time, he had been so self-absorbed, so overwhelmed with memories from past lives, that he had little left over for Carinja, whom his father had chosen and presented to him as a *fait accompli*. As he remembered, Carinja was as beautiful as Marika but duller, without the same intelligence and alertness. Walking along Mass. Ave. with Marike seemed somehow right and comfortable. "By the way," he said, "I don't blame your ancestor for leaving my ancestor four hundred years ago."

"Well that's a load off my mind."

"He was a drunkard, abusive, totally overwhelmed by his past."

"You sound as if you knew him," said Marike.

"That would make me more than fifteen."

"I ought to warn you, I don't go out with guys over four hundred."

They laughed and, on an impulse she couldn't explain to herself, she took Seth's arm.

"I guess you have to set *some* limits," said Seth.

As they walked, a black limousine followed them from a distance.

When they veered off Mass. Ave. and reached the first buildings of Adams House, one of the self-sufficient residences for upperclassmen, Marike took her arm from Seth's. "Well, this is me," she said. "Where are you?"

"With a family over on Brattle Street."

"How did you manage that?" asked Marike.

"They thought I was too young to associate with normal students. You might corrupt me."

"We'd certainly try," said Marike.

They stood facing each other for a moment. They were just about the same height and the proximity was irresistible. They kissed briefly and then Marike said, "But not tonight." She pointed to a window on the second floor. "Roommates."

"It'd be statutory rape anyway."

"I'd forgotten about that," said Marike.

Seth walked off, smiling. "Don't worry, I wouldn't turn you in."

Marike's suite was luxurious for a dorm, a holdover from when the Adams House suites were known as the Gold Coast and reserved for wealthy undergraduates. When she entered, one of her roommates, Lila Behrens, an overweight brunette who was both jolly and slovenly, was drinking a beer while engrossed in her computer.

"I hear you scored," said Lila, without looking up.

"What are you talking about?"

"You left the party with the genius kid," said Lila.

"How in the name of fuck did you know about that?"

"It's all over the internet."

"He just walked me home," said Marike. "That was it."

"How about the kiss?"

"Holy shit. Is that over the internet?"

"No, I saw it when I looked out the window," said Lila.

"And you haven't had time to post it."

"Not yet."

Marike grabbed a beer from the fridge and sat down next to Lila. "He said he recognized me from a picture of one of my distant ancestors, four hundred years ago."

"Well, that's an original line," said Lila.

"I thought so, too. He talked as if he knew her."

"So he's possibly crazy."

"Could be," said Marike. "But *good* crazy, *creatively* crazy."

"Oh well, that's different."

Marike sat back in her chair and sipped her beer. "I wonder what it'd feel like to sleep with a man who's four hundred years old."

"I have a feeling you're gong to find out," said Lila.

17

Walking back from Adams House along Mount Auburn Street, Seth was still glowing from the kiss and reflected that the thrill of a first kiss survived the centuries, whether he was male or female, barbarian or civilized. In cultures that didn't kiss, it was sometimes the first touch, or even the first smile. As long as it was mutual and not a commandment of the parents or culture. The first kiss with each new partner was exactly like his first kiss with Marike, something to be treasured and relived.

As he was walking, lost in the excitement of Marike's lips, the same car that had been following him before stopped in front of him. A large man jumped out.

"Mr. Russell," he said.

Seth turned to run and was stopped by a second man, even larger than the first, who held his arm.

"This way, please," said the first man. He gestured to the door of the limousine, opened to the back seat. The second man pushed him inside and covered his head with a hood.

"I was expecting this," said Seth.

The man riding in the back seat with him pushed Seth's head down so he wouldn't be seen. They drove for perhaps half an hour, starting and stopping with the lights and traffic. Seth's suspicion was that someone who knew about his many lives felt threatened by them. That probably meant the Church, most likely the Catholic Church.

The car stopped and the men took Seth into a room with no windows, no decorations and an opaque screen. There were two chairs, one in front of the screen, one behind, and a table. "Wait here, please," said the first man.

"Do I have a choice?" said Seth.

The men left without answering, locking the door behind them. Seth took out his cell phone, dialed 911 and spoke to the operator.

"Hello, 911? I've been kidnapped. I'm serious. Two guys grabbed me off the street, put a hood over my head and drove me here, wherever here is. They just forgot to take away my cell, so I'd have to say these guys aren't geniuses. Really, I'm serious. Can you trace this call to a location? You can? Good, send the police, I'll keep the phone on. Wait a minute, someone's coming ..."

The door opened and a figure that seemed to be dressed in black took his place in the chair behind the screen. When he spoke, it was the voice of an old man. His language was Latin, his accent medieval. "Are you the person known as Seth Russell?" he asked.

Seth responded in the Latin he learned as a Roman soldier in 30 B.C., in the army of Agrippa, under the overall command of Octavius. "Your accent is atrocious."

The old man responded in medieval Latin. "I learned it a long time ago, in Rome."

"You learned church Latin, which sounds vulgar to someone who knows classical Latin."

"So it's true," said the old man in English.

"What's true?"

"You know exactly what I'm talking about."

"I guess you've heard some rumors about me," said Seth, wondering if Dr. Olmsted had anything to do with this. "Don't believe them."

"I have to know if there's any truth to them."

"There isn't."

"Are you willing to state this in writing, and on videotape?"

"I'd have to know exactly what I'm stating."

"You'll be given a script," said the old man, sounding more and more sure of himself. This was a man accustomed to being obeyed, thought Seth.

"Before we discuss this, I'd like to know why you felt the need to kidnap me in this melodramatic fashion."

"For the sake of secrecy," said the old man.

"So my public statement will be just for the record, in case you need it."

"That is correct."

"And why do you need this statement?" asked Seth.

"I can't tell you that."

"Is it by any chance because you represent the Cardinal of Boston? I don't know his name. Or perhaps you're the Cardinal himself."

"Why would you think that?"

"Because the Catholic church regards reincarnation as a heresy. You have a stake in disproving it. It conflicts with your concept of heaven and hell as rewards and punishments for deeds in this life."

"That's true with all Christian faiths. And Moslems as well."

"True, but only the Catholics would go to these lengths to understand and stamp out heresy at the same time," said Seth. "Can you imagine the Episcopalians kidnapping someone on the street and taking them to a secret location? Can you imagine the Methodists caring whether I claimed I was reincarnated or not? If I talked too much, the Moslems would just kill me. The Jews would ignore me. But only the Catholics would take me seriously enough to question me. Before burning me at the stake, of course. An ancestor of mine already went through that."

"When was that?" asked the old man.

"In 1494, in Sweden. Usually, heretics were decapitated first. In my case they made an exception."

"The church no longer burns heretics," said the old man.

"The church still hires kidnappers – why not executioners as well?"

"I apologize for the kidnapping. From the way you acted at first, we didn't think you'd come voluntarily."

Seth wondered when the police would arrive. Or, seeing that they had been summoned to what was probably a church building, they had written it off as a hoax. In any case, he thought he'd play for time. This conversation was not uninteresting. "I'm not sure why you went to the trouble. There are thousands of people who claim they remember their past lives – I've interviewed some of them myself. Why have I been singled out?"

"We've interviewed others."

"But I'm the only one you believe."

"I didn't say that. This is just a fact finding interview."

This was bizarre. If there's one thing this *wasn't*, it was a fact finding interview. Still, he was intrigued. "Oh well then, ask away."

The old man hesitated, then asked questions in a more monotonous voice, as if he was reading from a list. "How is it that you speak so many languages fluently? How are you so intimately acquainted with so many cultures? How can you speak classical Latin? How can you speak a Lapp language that's extinct?"

"You mean Olof Sirma's reindeer song in Kemi. I sang that in grade school."

"You came to our attention when you were a child. Your song was written up in the press."

"The Kemi language is well documented," said Seth. "I don't know if I sang it correctly."

The old man's voice seemed tired. There was a rasp that appeared with each sentence. "So you studied an extinct language and learned how to speak it, or at least sing it, at the age of eight. In addition to speaking Chinese fluently without ever having a lesson."

"You've done some research."

The man behind the screen sighed, paused, and when he spoke again sounded discouraged. "I don't know what to think. Could you be the real thing?"

"I've told you I'm not," said Seth.

"You haven't been convincing."

"It makes no difference. If reincarnation exists, it merely postpones the day of judgment and the assignment of people to heaven or hell until the end of time. You needn't trouble changing your core beliefs. And if there's no reincarnation, you have no problem – your condemnation of people to eternal pain or eternal boredom can go on as planned."

The old man actually seemed to chuckle. "I've also thought that Heaven might be boring."

"All those Halleluiahs and Hosannas."

"Yes, that might drive me crazy."

The old man allowed his amusement to calm down and asked a question in a different voice. "Do you think what we do in this life makes a difference in the life to come?"

Seth was surprised. Wasn't that the whole point behind Christianity? But he took the question seriously. "I only know what I've read," he said. "But I've read that this life makes no difference whatsoever in what you become in the next. But it makes a difference in the decisions you make once you remember what you did before."

"You grow wiser."

"Not necessarily. But you have more experience to draw from. You remember your good deeds and your bad deeds. Your prejudices may take several lifetimes to overcome. For example, if you hate Jews in one life and become a Jew in another life, it might tend to change your perspective."

"Do you know what you'll be in the next life?"

"No. That's the catch," said Seth. "Now I have a question for *you*."

"Go ahead."

"Have you found anyone, anywhere, that convinced you of a previous life?"

"No one until you," said the man behind the screen.

"Has anyone come close?"

"Not one," said the old man. "They were all fakes."

"You examined professional psychics and the like?"

"All nonsense," said the man.

"Is the search worldwide?"

"Is the church worldwide?" came the instant retort. "The search is even more intense in Asia, where reincarnation is accepted and there are many claimants."

"I've heard that there's some meditation technique that helps people remember their past lives."

"In Hindu and Buddhist cultures," said the man behind the screen. "Of all the people who used these techniques and claimed to remember past lives, we haven't found one we're sure of. Some are still possible but none of them remembers more than one life back. We haven't found anyone like you."

Seth looked at his watch. The police should be close by this time, if they were coming at all. "And you're not even sure of *me*."

"We'd like you to talk to some of our more seasoned investigators. I could have them here first thing tomorrow morning."

"And I'm to stay in your custody until then …"

"Unfortunately …"

"What's more unfortunate is that the police should be knocking on your door just about now. I called them while I was waiting for you."

The old man sounded alarmed. "They didn't take your …"

"Goons are not known for their intelligence."

"Excuse me." The figure got up and left the room. Shortly afterwards, Seth's cell rang and he answered it. "Yes, I'm here," he said. "I'm not sure where – a room with no windows."

The old man returned behind the screen, extremely agitated. "Please tell them this was a big mistake. You don't want to press charges."

"On two conditions," said Seth, who now clearly had the upper hand and realized that the church could be useful. "You'll keep me informed on any possibilities worldwide. Anyone you think might be the real thing."

"Yes."

"And when you find someone who might be possible, you'll come to me in your true self, not behind a screen. We'll meet in a park, just the two of us, when you bring me your first report."

The man hesitated but then agreed. "Very well. You know how much this means …"

"Yes."

18

Marike made the first move, out of curiosity. She invited Seth for brunch in Boston, where they were less likely to be seen. Brunch seemed the safest time to meet, with the lowest sexual overtones. Marike had to admit she was attracted to Seth, and she *had* kissed him, although only goodnight, but she had no intention of carrying it further. For one, he was fifteen and she wasn't a pervert. For another, she could be arrested for pursuing him and kicked out of school if she was convicted, maybe even jailed. But there couldn't be any harm in talking to him over bagels and lox.

Somehow, Seth charmed her into letting him hold her hand, then caress her neck and, before she knew it, as if she had no will of her own, she found herself in a room with him in a sleazy hotel in downtown Boston. He hadn't attempted to seduce her in any way – in fact she was the one who suggested the hotel – but there was something in his manner that first intrigued and then excited her. He was like an older, sophisticated cosmopolite inside a boy's body. Even in the hotel, they made love in such slight, titillating stages that she was hardly aware they had graduated to real sex until she was already steaming with lust.

When they were finally satiated, she lay back in bed breathing heavily as if she had run a marathon. "My God, where did you learn all that?" she asked, panting.

"Church," said Seth. This was literally true. One of his earliest memories, one that was not quite well formed but still identifiable, was that of a temple prostitute in ancient Greece.

"I'd like to meet your pastor," said Marike. "That was fantastic."

"I can't believe you're so much like her," Seth reflected.

"Who?"

"Carinja."

"My ancestor?"

"The same rhythms, the same expressions." The resemblance between Carinja and Marika was uncanny, in particular during sex, at the beginning of their marriage, before the war with England. When he returned, crippled and embittered, even though he remembered countless lives, he was drinking heavily and impossible to live with. Marike was Carinja before the war.

Marike pulled the sheet over her breasts. "Seth, you're beginning to weird me out."

Seth shook his head back to reality. "No, I mean what I imagined Carinja to be like, from her portrait."

"You're still weird," Marike said. "Just not as much."

"I know. I tend to confuse things that I've read with reality. For example …"

He moved his hand over the sheet and down her body. "Here's something I learned from Lais of Corinth, a prostitute of the temple of Aphrodite in the 5th Century B.C., not the famous one, who was assassinated, an earlier one who died of alcoholism."

Marike was eager to learn.

19

In a dark coffee house on Mt. Auburn Street, a block away from Harvard Square, Marike and her roommate, Lila, Mary, Kelo, Clay and several other students who were reasonably close to Seth gathered around a table sipping cappuccinos or herbal teas. All, in one way or another, had been touched by the strange anomalies in Seth's behavior.

Marike was the first to bring up the subject. "So guys, what do you think?" she asked. "What are we dealing with here? A freak? An alien? A Bodhisattva?"

"I vote for the Bodhisattva," said Kelo.

"He's too cute to be an alien," said Lila.

"That's their disguise to put you off your guard," said Clay. "Underneath, he's all tubes and teeth."

"You didn't sleep with him, did you?" asked Mary.

Marike shrugged.

"How old is he, fifteen?" Clay commented.

"Well, that's the question," said Marike.

"There's no possible way he could be fifteen," said Kelo.

"Why do you say that?"

"Well, it's the language thing, for one." said Kelo. "He spoke to me in a click language that's almost impossible to learn without having lived in Botswana. Actually, he's so fluent he'd have to have been raised there. And he's never been to Africa at all. That's aside from the other languages he speaks with other foreign students, like Chinese and Dutch and Arabic."

"So what are you implying?" asked Marike.

"I don't know," Kelo admitted.

"You said it was a language thing, *for one*," said Marike. "What's another?"

"I can answer that," said Mary. "It's just a feeling. A self-confidence maybe. I mean, there are a lot of geniuses at Harvard, some even younger than Seth."

"You mean that math kid ... I don't know his name. Lives with his mother ... what is he thirteen, fourteen ...?"

"*That* one," said Mary. "But he's clearly a kid. A genius but a kid in every other way. Seth isn't a kid in any way."

"You're telling me," said Marike.

"Is he that good in bed?" said Lila.

"Well, he's not a kid."

"So what is he?" asked Mary.

They pondered this for a moment, sipped their drinks, and came up with no answers.

20

"I'm botching up," said Seth.

It was early evening in Dr. Olmsted's office. They were sitting not at Dr. Olmsted's desk but in easy chairs surrounding a coffee table where Olmsted tutored his most promising students. He had just poured a *Fino* into two sherry glasses and they clinked in a polite toast.

"What do you mean?" asked Olmsted.

"I'm botching this life, this opportunity. It's so different from any other age."

"So how are you botching up?"

"More and more people know about me," said Seth. "*You*, of course. The Catholic church thinks it knows about me. Many of the students, my friends, suspect something. And the other night I was with a girl and almost gave it away."

"You were with a girl?" said Olmsted, surprised.

"Does that surprise you?" said Seth. "With every life you get a new body and the hormones start pumping at puberty. Most of the time, I've been in a culture where you couldn't express yourself sexually, except along very narrow parameters. But it's definitely there. It slows down with age but not always."

"I somehow thought the urge would abate over the centuries."

"Sex doesn't abate. Love doesn't abate. What abates is craziness. You have emotions and urges but they don't control you. Well, most of the time."

"And the girl you were with the other night …"

"That's something I've never experienced before: her ancestor was my wife."

"How weird."

"That's what she said."

"You *told* her?"

"I fudged it," said Seth. "I said I'd seen a portrait of her ancestor in a gallery in Holland and it reminded me of her."

"Is there such a portrait?"

"No, I made it up," said Seth. "I think she thought it was an original line but she's suspicious."

"Do you like her?" asked Olmsted.

"I treated her ancestor very badly four hundred years ago. I'd like to make up for it."

Olmsted chuckled. This was turning out to be a very bizarre conversation. "She could be your great great great granddaughter."

"Actually, no, we never had children. Occasionally I've seen people who might have been related to me in another life – there are features and body types that repeat themselves over the generations. But this is the first time I've been certain."

Dr. Olmsted sat back and sipped his sherry. "So are you planning to mate with her, if you haven't already?"

"Oh yes, we've mated," said Seth. "But I don't think the distant relationship will make any difference. If I want a child who remembers his past incarnations, I'll probably have to mate with someone like me."

"Why is it so important?"

Seth seemed to bristle at the question. He sat up straighter and his voice became more intense. "Why is it so important to create a race that remembers? To create a race that sees through religion and patriotism and *honor* and *glory*, that understands the consequences of its actions?"

"I see your point."

"I remember reading a play by George Bernard Shaw where he argued that humans would have to live at least 300 years before they can overcome the pettiness, insanity and fatal egoism that's behind all wars and opposes all progress."

"*Back to Methuselah.*"

"Yes. But medical science may not achieve a life that long. Begetting a race that remembers its past lives may be more practical. I'd probably have to find someone like me."

"Do you have any guarantee that if you mate with someone like you, your children and grandchildren will remember their past lives?" asked Olmsted.

"No, but I have to try. Except that I can't search if I'm locked up in a nuthouse again. And the surest way to get locked up is to start boasting about how special I am."

"So from your point of view, letting this girl know about you is dangerous."

Seth nodded. "The problem is, I like her. And the hormones are still pumping." He sighed. "It'd be nice to fall in love again."

"Haven't you done that a hundred times?"

"Actually, no," said Seth. "The women or men I've been married to were usually arranged and romantic love was rarely a part of it. But I did love that Dutch girl who left me. That was one of the two lives I remember when I was an alcoholic and out of control, once as a man, once as a woman."

"It must get very confusing," said Olmsted.

"Not at all," said Seth. "Whether I'm tall, short, male, female, black, white or yellow, I'm always me. The sense of self is always there, once the memories return. What's confusing is the sheer volume of people I've loved – mothers and fathers, brothers and sisters, wives and children. I can't possibly keep track of them all, even the ones I've loved deeply."

"Don't you get hardened to it over the centuries?"

"Remember, my memories don't start until I'm seven or eight, so the bonding process has already started. Sometimes I'm overwhelmed with sadness at the people I've loved and lost …"

"Is there any way I can help?" asked Olmsted.

"It's just nice to have someone to talk to, to unload on, to put it bluntly. Now, how can I help *you*?"

Olmsted took out a large Xerox of a manuscript, with a wax seal at the bottom. "This seal …"

"The seal of Amu I-Hassan before he became Sultan of Grenada. What about it?"

"Thank you," said Olmsted.

"I was a physician then. I prescribed for him."

"What sort of prescription?" asked Olmsted.

"Nowadays, we'd call it a placebo."

21

few days later, Seth received a call from the old man of the church, possibly the Cardinal himself. He recognized the voice immediately and was relieved at the contact, which saved him from wondering about it.

They agreed to meet on the Boston Common, near the swan boats that afternoon. "How will I recognize you?" asked Seth.

"Sit on a bench – I'll recognize *you*."

At the appointed time, Seth noticed the two goons from before, now dressed in the black robes of priests. On a bench nearby, though not within listening distance, sat a man who looked to be in his late 70's or early 80's, also in a black robe with no indication of his position. It was not the Cardinal of Boston – Seth had googled him – but he may have been the Cardinal of somewhere else. He had the look and demeanor of someone important. As Seth approached, he remained seated but held Seth's eyes in his and nodded.

"You wanted to meet without the screen between us," said the man, with a slight smile.

Seth returned the smile. "What do I call you?" he asked.

The old man seemed confused at first but recovered quickly. "Why don't you address me as 'Father Doe?'"

"Why are you still keeping your identity a secret?"

"For your protection, my son."

Seth grimaced. "Very well, but I'm not your son."

"I know. I have an assignment for you." He handed Seth a folder.

"What's this?"

"You wanted to find someone like you, who remembers his past lives," said Father Doe. "We may have found someone."

Seth opened the folder and gazed at the first page. "In India?"

"The man is quite a celebrity in his part of India," said Doe. He has an ashram in Andhra Pradesh, which seems to be some kind of rehab center for Bollywood celebrities."

"Not a sterling recommendation."

"He claims to remember all his lives back to when he was a monkey in the jungle."

"At least he's read Darwin," said Seth.

"The problem is, nobody's been able to trip him up. Our people have tried and failed."

Seth examined the first page of the report. "Swami Pralada?"

"Named for some character in their scriptures."

Seth flipped through the document, which was only three pages long. When he remarked that it wasn't very comprehensive, Father Doe asked him to make a report of his own.

"You mean go to India?" asked Seth.

"We'd pay your expenses."

"What language do they speak in Andhra Pradesh? I've never been there."

"Telegu."

"Unfortunately I don't know it. It's not related to Hindi or Urdu but I hear it's a beautiful language – every word ends in a vowel."

"Will you meet with him?" asked Father Doe.

Seth hesitated. It seemed like such a wild goose chase. He didn't trust men who led ashrams any more than he trusted the leaders of megachurches. Then again, he hadn't been to India in over five hundred years – it'd be interesting to see how the place had changed. "I could do it over the Christmas break. Would that suit you?"

22.

"I 'll see you the 23rd, then you're with your family Christmas Eve and Christmas Day, then you're off to India," said Marike.

They were on the train to New York, just entering the tunnel to Grand Central Station.

"You've memorized my schedule," said Seth, jokingly.

"You still haven't told me why you're going to India."

"I told you."

"No, you just lied," said Marike. She had entered that stage in a relationship where lies were no longer charming or funny. Marike really wanted to know why Seth was going.

"It's too cold in New York," said Seth.

"You're going for the weather ..."

"I thought it'd be a nice place to go," offered Seth.

"What's the big secret anyway?"

"I'm going to interview a Hindu swami for the diocese of Boston."

"Okay, *don't* tell me," said Marike, slightly annoyed. "Keep it a mystery."

They spent the next day together, wandering, seeing the Christmas windows, skating at Rockefeller Center, gawking at Tiffany's, and window shopping, with a passionate interlude at a hotel on 10th Avenue. Introducing each other to their parents was not possible due to the age gap, so they had only part of a day to be together, lying to both sets of parents about the time they would arrive home.

Marike was unquestionably smitten with Seth, perhaps even in love with him. They were an unlikely couple, she knew, and probably no one would understand the attraction, except that of a predatory woman with an innocent boy, if fifteen year old boys could be considered innocent. On the street, they couldn't hold hands or kiss or even exchange meaningful glances. The pretense was that of brother and older sister. Perhaps when Seth was of legal age, they could relax but for now, Seth couldn't pass for legal. Although his voice had changed and he had enough facial hair to shave, he didn't look particularly old for his age, except for his expression.

They parted at a storage facility near Penn Station, where they had stowed their luggage for the day. The problem was finding some place to kiss goodbye. Fortunately, the storage facility was on the 2nd floor of an office building but unfortunately, on the way up there was a man in the elevator with them. On the way down, they had the elevator to themselves and exchanged a brief, passionate kiss that left them both breathless.

23

The trip to India was brief and unproductive, although getting there was anything but brief. He took a plane to Mumbai, which connected to a plane for Hyderabad, which connected to a flight to Ahobilam, where he boarded a bus to Swami Prahlada's ashram.

The bus dropped him off at an ornate arch, decorated with statues of Hindu deities, topped by a mystical symbol Seth didn't recognize. This led to a wide path of tiles, under another arch leading to a building that looked like a cross between a temple and a hotel. At the entrance, Seth gave his name to a humorless acolyte who directed him to a meditation area in a courtyard of the building, within a formal garden.

Prahlada looked every inch a swami, a short, lively man in his 60's with a white beard and long hair tied in a bun. When Seth arrived he was in the lotus position under a Banyan tree, conducting a lesson for a group of disciples. At Seth's appearance, he stopped the session to greet his visitor.

"You must be Mr. Russell," he said. The disciples turned to look.

"Yes."

"I'm ready for your inquisition," he said, in a friendly voice, utterly at ease. He spoke with a slight accent and evinced no surprise at Seth's age.

"I'm afraid I didn't bring the usual instruments of torture," said Seth. Prahlada laughed. "As you know, I have been sent by the Catholic church to interview you, but I'm not a member of the church. In fact, I actively dislike organized religions of every faith."

"So do I," said Prahlada. "So how did the church entice you to question me?"

"Their purposes and my purposes coincided."

"Ah," said Prahlada, smiling. "The church wants to explode the myth of karma by denying the truth of reincarnation. Is that also your purpose?"

Seth laughed. "Our purposes don't coincide on that point. I'm not here to determine the truth of karma or reincarnation, just to determine the truth of *your* incarnations. And for that, I need a private audience, away from your disciples."

"I have nothing to hide from anyone," said Prahlada.

"But *I* do," said Seth.

Prahlada regarded him quizzically. "You are a teenage American boy, yet you represent the largest religious organization in the world. Interesting."

He guided Seth to a gazebo on the property and chatted with him for over an hour. He was cheerful, positive, upbeat and without any mystical mumbo-jumbo that characterized most people who make outlandish claims. He was not bashful about describing his past lives and happily answered Seth's questions in a forthright manner, which seemed entirely convincing. Except that Seth was not convinced.

In the airport for the return trip, he texted Father Doe and voiced his suspicions. "I can't definitely disprove Prahlada's claims but the past lives that he talks about are all from the same area and all in the same language. He's a bit fuzzy with details but I wasn't able to catch him up on historical events or figures, mainly because all of the lives he claims were away from historical events. I think he's faking but I can't prove it. He may actually believe he remembers things that he just made up, the way people under hypnosis do. Actually, I think he's hypnotized himself into creating a series of past lives that can't be verified. It's good for convincing disciples though. I'll write you more when I get back."

He was not prepared for what he faced on the way home.

24

is trip to India was his first flight on an airplane and he had found it astonishing. He had known about planes in several lives but to actually ride in one was a thrill he never expected. On the way home, he made sure he had a window seat and sat glued to the window as the plane took off and rose into the air. It was something he had never experienced in any other life (although he had dreamed of it in several) and he found it mesmerizing.

When he had finally calmed down from the thrill of flying, he opened his laptop and prepared to outline a paper that was due the next week. But first he checked his list of emails, which he expected to be large because he had not been able to get an internet connection at the ashram.

The first one, at the top of the screen, was from someone he didn't know. It said, "CONTACT ME IMMEDIATELY," in all caps.

The next one down was more informative, if absurd: "WE KNOW YOU ARE THE ONE!" He had no idea what they were talking about.

The next, also in all caps: "GOD CURSES YOU."

Another: "Are you the one?"

"BLASPHEMER"

"We need to talk."

"BURN IN HELL"

"I loved you 150 years ago." Now this was beginning to make sense. Obviously, his cover was blown.

"GOD PUNISHES LIARS!!!"

"Why have you returned?"

His plane landed at JFK since he was returning to his parent's apartment in New York for the remainder of the Christmas break. He had no baggage other than a light backpack and sailed through passport control and customs. As he passed through the gate into the arrivals hall, a young man approached him. "Are you the one?" he asked.

"No," said Seth quickly and walked on.

Almost immediately, he was approached by two young women.

"Are you Seth Russell?" said one.

"No, he's back there," said Seth, gesturing behind him.

As the women turned to the gate, Seth escaped as quickly as he could.

He arrived at his parent's apartment building to find a crowd outside, a mix of middle-aged and young people, shivering in the cold. There was snow on the ground and a large wreath on the front door. Inside one could see Christmas lights. A stalwart doorman, George, whom Seth had known all his life, guarded the entrance and tried to keep the crowd from blocking the door.

Seth strolled up to the man farthest away from the entrance. "What's going on?" he asked.

"The immortal lives here."

"The what?"

"The immortal, a man who has been among us for thousands of years."

"You're kidding," said Seth.

"We have it on the highest authority."

"What's that?"

"The Catholic Church has been covering it up for centuries. But one of their priests went public."

"So this guy is a thousand years old?" asked Seth.

"Older."

"Must be hard to get a date," said Seth, and walked off. He phoned his parents, who were well aware of the crowd and who had been inundated with phone calls until they turned off their landline and relied only on their cells. He thought he'd try staying with Marike's family, if they'd let him.

25

He spent the remainder of his break at Marike's, which was a bit awkward, even after he explained to her parents that this was an emergency. They had separate rooms, of course, and no intimacy was even intimated, but her parents were suspicious. They were also excited to be hiding a fugitive from a horde of crazed would-be disciples. And fascinated by Seth's knowledge of their ancestor in 17th Century New Amsterdam. Seth's parents came by several times and once with Greg on New Year's Day. The crowd had disbanded by that time but they weren't sure it was safe to return to their apartment.

Back in Cambridge, a small group had camped on the lawn of his house on Brattle Street. As often as the police chased them away, they returned in the hope of seeing Seth. Eventually, Seth petitioned Harvard for a new identity.

"You know, I've had to move to a new family," he explained to Professor Olmsted."

"I didn't."

"I have a new name. Harvard agreed to let me change it to Pierre Reynard, a French student studying American literature."

"Well, you speak French," said Olmsted.

"I speak 18th Century French – I have to update my vocabulary, not to mention my slang and my accent. So I have a new address, with a family on Garden Street, a new email, a new cell number, everything."

"You can't hide indefinitely," said Olmsted.

"I know," said Seth. "I'll have to deal with it eventually. The good side is that being notorious might just attract another person like me. It's just a question of sorting out all the letters and emails addressed to Seth Russell."

"How many do you get?"

"So far about a hundred. Mostly from people who think I'm the Messiah or people who think I'm the Devil. A lot of them want to tell me about their past lives, some say they knew me five hundred years ago, one woman is convinced I was her husband in Rumania, another remembered that I had raped her in 1,300 B.C. and wanted compensation."

"Did you?" asked Olmsted.

"When I was a Roman soldier, we were expected to rape women but I was already beyond that – I simulated rape a few times. But that would have been around 30 B.C. in our calendar. I have no idea what 1,300 B.C. corresponded to in my lives. I was raped myself a couple of times, including marital rape two lives ago. Of course, it wasn't called *rape*, it was called *duty,* or *submission.* One submits to one's husband as he submits to God. The fact that I didn't submit to it willingly meant that I was probably a heretic and should be punished."

Professor Olmsted knew all about these attitudes but he was still shocked by the reality. To actually know somebody who had been legally raped and whose rape had been blessed by an all-knowing and "merciful" deity was different from just reading about it. But when he thought about it, raping an immortal was different from raping a mortal, who had no choice but to endure or kill herself. "Why didn't you kill yourself and go to another life?"

"I thought about it," said Seth. "But the next life might have been worse. I could have been tortured like in Sweden or die horribly like in Bandiagara or have the skin of my face removed like among the Shuar headhunters of the Amazon. The curse of being immortal is that in every life I'm mortal. My mortality is intensified by having to go through it over and over again."

"I had suspected that immortality wasn't entirely a blessing," said Olmsted. "But given the alternative ..."

"The alternative might be a blessing as well," said Seth. "But that doesn't solve the immediate problem, how to deal with a group of crazies who want to worship me."

They discussed several strategies, none of them practical. If he lied to them, they wouldn't believe him. If he told the truth, they would never let him alone. If he ran away, they'd find him. If he denied everything, they'd bedevil him. If he killed himself, he might wake up to something worse.

"So what are you going to do?" asked Olmsted.

"I'm going to sleep on it," said Seth.

"With Marike?"

"Of course."

26

With difficulty, Seth managed to make it to Marike's dorm without being followed by a crazy – at least he didn't notice anyone. Finally, they were able to make love in comparative privacy and took full advantage of it. Lila, Marike's roommate, despite her innate nosiness, left them alone in Marike's room and turned up the music on her stereo to drown out the sounds.

They had been in the room for perhaps an hour when Lila knocked on the door.

"Marike, Seth, get dressed," she shouted.

Before the couple could respond, the door to the room was opened and a young, attractive policewoman entered the room.

"Marike Biekman?" she asked.

Marike responded from under the covers. "Yes?"

"Would you get dressed, please?"

Marike got out of bed naked and reached for her clothes on the floor. Seth made a move to leave the bed as well.

"Stay where you are," said the policewoman. "A policeman will be here while you get dressed."

"What's this about?" asked Marike.

The policewoman addressed Seth. "Are you Seth Russell?"

Seth assumed that his new name, Pierre Reynard, hadn't filtered down to officialdom. "Yes," he responded.

The policewoman called to someone outside the door. "He's in here."

Fully clothed, they gathered in the common room. Only Lila was still in her bathrobe. The policewoman took Marike's arm. "Marike Biekman, you are under arrest for statutory rape. You have the right to remain silent. Anything you say can and will be used against you in a court of law."

111

"You're kidding," said Marike.

"You have the right to an attorney. If you cannot afford an attorney, one will be appointed to you. Do you understand these rights as they have been read to you?"

"I don't understand anything," said Marike.

"You don't have to understand why you've been arrested," said the policewoman. "You just have to give some indication that you understand your rights."

"Okay, I understand them," said Marike, testily.

The policeman, who had the air of a frat boy, turned to Seth. "May I see your I.D.?" He looked at it and seemed puzzled. "It says Pierre Reynard."

"Harvard allowed me to attend school under an assumed name, to avoid nosy people."

"I understand," said the policeman. "I've heard of you myself. Can you verify your age for me?"

"I told Marike I was eighteen."

The policeman was about to respond when his phone buzzed. "Yes, sir," he said into his phone. "They're both here. We're bringing them in now. Yeah, the victim, too."

"Victim?" said Seth. He had forgotten that most Americans considered him beneath the age of consent, incapable of making a rational decision.

Meanwhile, the policewoman got out her handcuffs and told Marike to put her hands behind her back. "What if I have to sneeze?" said Marike.

"Just put them behind your back," she said and cuffed Marike, who remarked, "This is surreal."

The policeman told Seth, "We'd like you to come down, too, to give your statement."

"I don't have a statement," said Seth.

"Well then, to answer a few questions."

"I don't have any answers either," said Seth. "Out of curiosity, who's the complainant?"

"You'll find out in due time."

"Is it one of those people who think I'm God. Or one of those people who think I'm Satan?"

"Actually, I don't know," said the policeman, genially.

"Somebody get me a lawyer," said Marike.

"I don't know any lawyers," said Lila.

"I'll find one," said Seth.

"This is crazy," said Marike as the policewoman led her out.

27

Seth and Marike spent the night in the police station. While Seth was questioned, he admitted nothing, refusing to answer most of the pertinent questions. During this process, Marike was locked in a cage for women, which normally held prostitutes, crazies and real criminals but was fortunately empty this night. Seth was released around three am and picked up by the man from his new family, since they couldn't let a juvenile go home on his own.

The next day, they transferred Marike to the D.A.'s office. Her parents had flown up from New York with Sidney Berenson, the family lawyer. Horace Barnes, the Assistant D. A. in charge of the case, was short, florid, wore bow ties and looked utterly anachronistic, like a holdover from the 19th Century. Along with his assistant, a young woman who seemed slightly lost, they gathered around a table, sipping coffees and teas from plastic cups.

Mrs. Biekman was just as incredulous as Marike about the reason for this meeting. "I don't understand. If the boy isn't pressing charges and his parents aren't pressing charges, who *is* pressing charges?"

"The state of Massachusetts," said Barnes. "Acting on a tip, we caught your daughter in bed with a 15-year-old child."

"A tip from who?" asked Mrs. Biekman.

"A concerned citizen."

"This is a witch hunt," said Mr. Biekman.

"Seth isn't a child," said Marike.

"I know, he told you he was eighteen," said Barnes, cynically.

"Actually, he didn't."

Barnes glanced at some papers handed to him by his assistant. "Our records say he's fifteen. How old do you think he is?"

"At least four hundred and fifty years old," Marike shot back, without a pause.

"Don't be ridiculous," said Mrs. Biekman.

"That's absurd," her father seconded.

"He hasn't out and out told me but he's left so many indications that it's impossible to think otherwise."

Barnes turned his attention to Marike's parents. "I think you have to understand, a religious cult has grown up around this boy. Somehow, he's convinced a great many gullible people, including your daughter, that he's some kind of Jesus figure, risen from the dead."

"That's not it at all," said Marike.

Berenson, the Biekman's lawyer, thought that this would change the nature of the case.

"Not really," said Barnes. "The boy would have to prove in court that he was more than fifteen."

"He may be fifteen in this life," said Marike. "But this is one of many lives."

"I think the law recognizes only one life but if I'm not mistaken, you've just admitted to statutory rape," said Barnes.

"She admitted nothing at all," said Berenson, knowing she had. "She's clearly under the influence of a magnetic personality who's using her for his own ends."

"Oh for God's sake," said Marike.

Barnes offered a deal. "Let's 'just make this easy on all of us. She pleads guilty, we'll offer her a minimal sentence and recommend suspension, since it's her first offence."

Berenson pretended to be shocked. "A guilty plea means she'll be listed as a sex offender."

When Barnes shrugged, Mr. Biekman added, "And she'll be thrown out of college."

"She broke the law," said Barnes. "Admittedly, we were tipped off by other members of his cult, but we did catch them red-handed, *in flagrante delicto*, naked in bed."

Marike didn't argue the point. She pouted. "It's not a cult."

Berenson looked at Barnes, as if to say, *see what I mean?*

"So what's your suggestion?" asked Barnes.

"Just drop it."

"You know I can't do that," said Barnes. "Charges have been filed. The boy is a minor, five years younger than the defendant. The state of Massachusetts assumes Ms. Biekman took advantage of Mr. Russell's youth and inexperience for her own ends."

Marike was outraged. "That is so ridiculous, I can't even …"

Barnes was adamant. "We're a nation of laws."

Berenson attempted to rise to the occasion. "So you're saying the only way Marike can avoid being kicked out of college and being branded a sex offender for the rest of her life is to take our chances on a trial by jury."

"I'm offering no jail time versus a possible seven years in jail. Theoretically, she could get life, so this seems to me like a generous offer."

"I won't take it," said Marike.

Marike's mother thought they should think about it, which irritated Marike. "I would never take advantage of a child," Marike said. "I'm not going to admit I did."

"This could be dangerous," said Berenson.

"Don't worry about it." said Marike. "If we put Seth on the stand, everyone will understand."

Berenson raised his eyebrows while Marike's father said simply, under his breath, "Oh my god."

"Give me your answer tomorrow," said Barnes.

28

Back in his room the day following Marike's arrest, Seth spent several hours on his homework and then got down to the arduous task of reading and possibly answering his emails. There were nearly 100 of these, mostly from crazies wanting his advice or blessing, some cursing him for made-up offences or praising him for made-up deeds. Some gave him useful advice like, "Rot in hell, Judas" or "Get a life, scumbag." Eventually he finished the emails with a wave of disgust and started on his snail mail, which was more of the same:

> My mother has cancer. Her doctors hold out no hope but I have hope since I read about you …

> You are a disgrace to the human race, commie asshole bastard …

> Heavenly Father, have mercy on us, poor sinners …

He tossed these aside and was about to throw the whole pile in the waste basket when one caught his eye. It was in a brown envelope postmarked Papua New Guinea and pretty much the worse for wear, rumpled, stained and partially open. It was addressed by hand, in excellent penmanship reminiscent of an earlier era, to his parent's address in New York, redirected to his first Harvard address, then to this address.

He read it with growing excitement. It had been written six years ago and referenced the performance in his elementary school when he sang a song in Kemi, the extinct Sami language of Finland. It was just possible that the writer of this letter was the real thing. He rang Professor Olmsted and met him in his study.

"Listen to this," he said to Olmsted.

> "I don't know when this will reach you, if at all, but I felt I must write. Word of a boy who speaks an extinct Kemi language has spread to the remote highlands of Sandaun Province in Papua New Guinea, where I live."

"The postmark confirms it," said Seth. "Just look at the stamps on the envelope. Have you ever seen stamps like these?" The stamps were quite spectacular: a warrior with an elaborate headdress in orange, green, white and yellow, a montage of smiling children wearing face paint, a tribal mask, a ferocious warrior with a bone through his nose. "I've never seen anything like them."

"Go on," said Olmsted.

> "I'm in a clan situation which doesn't permit much contact with the outside world but I get reports from time to time and I've found a willing missionary to post this letter for me when he returns to what passes for civilization in this part of the world. (That would be Port Moresby – I've never been there but I hear it's one of the worst cities in the world, hazy with smoke and riddled with crime. But at least it has a post office.)"

"He doesn't sound like he lives in the bush," said Olmsted.
"*She.*"
"Well, she seems to have a civilized perspective."
'Unquestionably."

> "Allow me to introduce myself. My present name is Ybunlis. I am a priestess of Yuwan, a god who never intervenes in the affairs of men except through his priestesses. This makes me the local shaman in Mindanna, an Oksapmin village in the Telefomin District of Sandaun Province in Papua New Guinea. Despite my remote location and

unlikely occupation, I believe we have something in common."

"Is this for real?" asked Olmsted.

"Listen."

"I, too, speak, read and write an extinct language, Etruscan ..."

"My God," said Olmsted.

"... which had a rich literary tradition, now completely lost. How do I know Etruscan, or English for that matter? The same way you know Kemi, or English."

"This must be a joke," said Olmsted.

"The same way I'm a joke," said Seth.

"Good point."

"Anyway, it goes on:"

"We must meet. I don't have the money to visit you so you must come to me. Assuming you're still in New York, you can take Qantas to Port Moresby, then an Air Niugini flight to Vanimo and a connecting MAF or VanAir flight to Telefomin. From there you could get a guide and walk to Oksapmin. Or I could have someone meet you there, if I know you're coming. Or you could hike to my village, Mindanna, which is about a day's walk from Oksapmin.

"I have been disappointed in the past but if we really have this in common, you know how important it is to meet.

"Very truly yours, Ybunlis, wife of Gwe, priestess of Yuwan."

"Very strange," said Olmsted, after a long pause.

"Is it possible?" mused Seth.

Neither spoke for a minute, contemplating a civilized priestess in a savage land, until Seth absent-mindedly turned over the letter. "Wait a minute, there's something on the other side."

It was a postscript that began, "This may help convince you that I am what you are." The sentence was repeated in 10 languages. He showed them to Olmsted. "Arabic, Swedish, Chinese … I don't know this one but it could be some Mayan language, translated into Roman script."

"This must be Etruscan," said Olmsted, pointing to one sentence.

"The alphabet is similar to Phoenician."

"You must meet with her as soon as possible," said Olmsted.

"I have Marike's trial coming up."

"Do you have to appear?"

Seth smiled and nodded. "If you only have one life and you do something dishonorable, you only have to live with it for a few years. If you have many lives, you have to live with it for centuries. I would never forgive myself if I didn't show up for her trial."

"I see your point," said Olmsted.

"The danger is, if I deny everything, she goes to jail and that's the end of her life. If I convince the jury that I'm four hundred years old, that's the end of *my life* – I'm harried by fanatics or sent to a nuthouse, or both. What would *you* do?"

"I'm old fashioned," said Olmsted. "I'd be a gentleman and ruin my life."

"Even if you'd lose a valuable historical resource …"

"You'll be back in another form," said Olmsted. "You'll remember me."

"I think you're right. But maybe I can convince the jury another way."

29

Later on that day, Seth got in touch with Father Doe and they agreed to meet on Boston Common once again. They meandered along a path, followed at a discrete distance by his two goons.

"This may surprise you," said Father Doe, "but your Ybunlis is in our database. Ten years ago, someone brought word of a woman in the jungle, a sorceress supposedly, who spoke English with an upper class Victorian accent. We made a note of it but didn't follow up. Do you really think she's the one?"

"Enough to travel to New Guinea," said Seth. "Her letter was very convincing."

"I thought so, too," said Father Doe. "But I'm not sure I want it to be true."

Father Doe seemed genuinely disturbed. "Imagine the effect a positive proof of reincarnation would have on my church, on every denomination of Christianity, as well as Islam and perhaps Judaism."

"As I said before, reincarnation needn't negate heaven and hell and the day of judgment. It would just postpone it."

"You're being too rational. The effect would be catastrophic."

"And yet you have to know," said Seth.

"Yes," said Father Doe. "The church has to know the truth and then suppress it."

"You're not serious. Isn't that like the Grand Inquisitor in *The Brothers Karamazov* who is faced with the second coming of Christ and puts him in prison. Would you have your church based on a lie?"

"Religious truth is tested by what effect it has on people, not by how literally it adheres to a set of facts," said Father Doe. "We can't prove much of what the Bible says – we take it on faith. But it's faith that makes the difference, that gives people hope, that makes them strive for goodness, that teaches them love and forgiveness."

"It seems to teach them hate and intolerance as well," said Seth.

"I can't deny that. But most people, I think, want to live a good life, and the church helps them. At least in theory – I know it doesn't always work out like that."

"And you think incontrovertible proof of reincarnation would disillusion the faithful."

"I think the disillusionment would rock the church to its foundations. I don't know if Christianity would survive."

"Why should it?" said Seth. "Zeus didn't survive. Isis and Osiris didn't survive, although they went on longer than Christianity. Ishtar's gone. Odin, Quetzacoatl, Enlil … A lot of the crazies out there think *I'm* God."

"Yes, I've heard," said Father Doe, with a hint of a smile.

"So even if I rock the church to its foundations, you'll still pay for my trip to New Guinea?"

"Of course. We can do damage control when you get back. When do you want to leave?"

"Right after the trial," said Seth.

"The trial worries me," said Father Doe. "All that publicity."

"I think you'll enjoy it," said Seth.

30

arike's trial was held in the Cambridge District Court, a modern building in Medford, not close to Harvard Square and utterly inconvenient, but still in the Cambridge district.

Marike had insisted on a jury trial against the advice of her lawyer, Sidney Berenson, and her parents. Horace Barnes, the Assistant District Attorney prosecuting Marike, had no doubt about the outcome of the trial, which was unfortunate – he didn't want to ruin the girl's life but there seemed to be no other way.

The judge, Herman Landau, was a dark, hawk-faced man in his 50's who seemed perpetually irritated. The courtroom was filled with spectators, including Mr. and Mrs. Biekman, Professor Olmsted, a representative of the church (not Father Doe) in priestly garb, Lila, Mary Wang, Kelo, Clay and other Harvard classmates, and a coterie of religious crazies, who were waiting to catch a glimpse of The Master and catch what words of wisdom issued from his immortal mouth.

But first, they had to sit through Horace Barnes' spiel on the definition and seriousness of statutory rape, to a few anonymous giggles among the spectators, and the prospect of hearing utter nonsense from the defense. Sidney Berenson, the defense attorney, decided to confront the religious aspect head on, portraying Marike as a victim rather than a predator. He also decided that Marike would not take the stand, as he felt she was likely to convict herself.

Barnes felt this was a simple, straight forward case. He had the two arresting offices describe responding to an anonymous phone tip, and the circumstances of the arrest, finding Marike and Seth in bed together unclothed. Berenson questioned them on a technicality – were they caught in the act of penetration, or in physical contact? The policeman and woman had to admit they hadn't witnessed any outright sexual activity. Both Berenson and Barnes knew this was a fudge area – it might or might not be meaningful to a jury.

Barnes emphasized the youth of the victim, the fact that he had not yet achieved his full growth, had only just begun to shave regularly, his voice had only changed recently, that Seth was in every way a juvenile, albeit a book-smart one. He was well below the age of consent, which should have been obvious to Marike just from looking at him, regardless of what age he claimed to be. Besides, his age was a matter of record. He produced Seth's birth certificate as the final, incontrovertible proof that Seth was a minor, who by definition, could not understand what he was forced to do.

"The poor boy," said one of the spectators to his neighbor, "forced to sleep with a beautiful woman."

Berenson countered with a courtroom circus. He brought in nearly a dozen crazies who testified that Seth was anywhere from four hundred to several thousand years old. Their answers to his questions ranged from merely fanciful to out-and-out deranged, like the young man with an ankh tattoo on his cheek who said Seth was from the planet, Krypton. And no, he did not believe that Krypton was a fictional planet dreamed up by the creators of Superman. Judge Landau told him to step down without allowing cross examination.

The sanest witnesses were Hindus and Buddhists who viewed reincarnation as the natural order of the universe. They saw no reason why Seth couldn't be thousands of years old in various forms. The Buddhist speculated that Seth could have been a man, an animal, a ghost, a demon and an angel in various incarnations. "Why is that more difficult to believe than heaven or hell?" he asked.

"It's my understanding that there's a period of forty-nine days between births," said Berenson.

"That's what many people believe," said the Buddhist. "After death we are confronted with karmic projections that help determine our next birth."

"So Seth could have been say, a cat, in his past life, and his deeds as a cat could have helped him become a human in this life."

"It's possible," said the Buddhist.

"Your witness," Berenson to Barnes.

"I'll pass," said Barnes.

Another witness thought that Seth had miraculous powers, among them mind control. Could he control Marike's mind? Berenson asked. Not just Marike's, said the witness, but the judge and jury. He was certain that Marike had no will of her own in the presence of a man with godlike powers. Once again, Barnes did not dignify this witness with a cross examination.

"I fail to see what case you're building," said Judge Landau, "but I'd like you to wrap it up right after lunch. We'll take a break until two."

The case Berenson was building was actually clear to both Landau and Barnes. He was trying to overwhelm the jury with possibilities, absurd or otherwise, that Marike could have faced in her relationship with Seth. Was he a god, a reincarnated Lothario, a mind controller, a Kryptonite, an ageless creature in a human body, a diabolical seducer from the dark side, etc. etc.? As Barnes was sure to point out, it didn't make any legal difference who Marike thought she was sleeping with, but it might make a difference to the jury.

In the afternoon, Berenson brought Seth to the witness stand. The disciples in the court were rapt, breathless, waiting for the wisdom of the ages. Barnes immediately objected. In a private conference with the judge and Berenson, Barnes complained that Seth had been listed as a prosecution witness and not a witness for the defense. Judge Landau ruled that Seth should be questioned by Barnes before Berenson. "I'm sure you were aware that the prosecution was on record as listing Mr. Russell as a prosecution witness," said the judge. Berenson apologized. Landau warned him against "funny stuff" and theatrics. Clearly, the judge favored Barnes, thought Berenson.

Since Seth had already been sworn in, it was Barnes who stood before Seth and looked at his notes, savoring the anticipation of the crowd.

"This trial has gone on for several hours and we've heard reams of testimony, mostly about *you*," said Barnes to Seth.

"I've been on a bench outside the courtroom so I haven't heard anything," said Seth.

"Well, it's been pretty fantastic," said Barnes. "The witnesses called by the defense have told us that you're either four hundred years old, or a thousand, or you've lived half a dozen lives, or maybe you're from another planet ..."

Berenson objected. "Your honor, is this getting anywhere?"

"Make your point, Counselor," said Landau.

Barnes stood directly in front of Seth when he asked his question. "Mr. Russell, how old are you in *this* life?"

"Fifteen."

"Thank you. No further questions."

In his mind, and hopefully in the jury's mind, the case was settled.

Barnes sat down and Berenson took his place. "If you're fifteen, how have you managed to persuade so many people that you're older?"

"I'm good with languages."

"Did you ever tell Ms. Biekman, or imply, that you were older than fifteen?"

"Of course," said Seth.

"Would you elaborate?"

"It's a little creepy," said Seth, who had decided to play the part of a somewhat twisted, semi-perverted predator.

"I'm sure the court won't mind."

"I first saw her in a coffee shop. I asked about her, found out her name and a little about her and looked up her background online. When I saw her later at a party, I pretended I was seeing her for the first time and got a friend to introduce us."

"Go on."

"So when we met, I made up some weird story about my ancestor being married to her ancestor to get her interest."

"You made up this story?"

"Yes, of course. Once I found out about her ancestor online, I concocted this ridiculous story about our connection. Then I threw out some hints that the connection might have been *me* in another life."

"Was there any truth to this?"

"None."

"Do you think she believed you?"

Seth smiled, with just a hint of slyness. Then he shrugged. "People will believe anything if you keep at it. At first she thought it was nonsense, which it was, but after a few more hints, and after other students started wondering about me, I think she actually believed that I was four hundred years old."

"And why did you do this?" asked Berenson.

"To make Marike like me."

"Wait a minute," said Berenson, looking at the jury. "We're not talking about some groupie or some cultist. We're talking about a physics major at Harvard, who had been Valedictorian of her high school class and a National Merit Scholar. Why would she buy such an elaborate hoax?"

"Because it's not so far-fetched. I speak over twenty languages, I have a photographic memory for historical detail and a vivid imagination. I'd have been surprised if she *didn't* believe me."

"Were you aware that Ms. Biekman might be charged with statutory rape if she consented to sleep with you?"

Seth was prepared for this. "I'm aware that the law says statutory rape may be an offense with or without knowledge of the victim's age. And I know that consent is not a defense. But what I perpetrated on Ms. Biekman was an out-and-out fraud. It requires a separate opinion."

Berenson turned to Judge Landau. "Believe it or not, your Honor, I didn't coach this witness in any way."

Landau admitted that he had never come across anyone like this. "Anything else, Mr. Russell?" he asked.

"Yes, your Honor," said Seth. "I believe the statutory rape law for children over fourteen but under sixteen – in other words, *me* – specifies that sexual intercourse, unnatural intercourse or abuse has to have occurred. None of this has been proven in this case. The fact that the police found us undressed does not imply anything other than consensual nudism. We were not caught in the act of anything, she was not examined at a hospital for signs of penetration and there is not the slightest evidence that we were doing anything at all."

"This is absurd," Barnes said, under his breath, shaking his head with disgust.

Berenson felt somewhat miffed that Seth had stolen his thunder. He had intended to bring this out gradually so that the jury could savor every new revelation. He thought he noticed an amused glance from the judge but perhaps he was mistaken.

"Can I say one thing more?" Seth asked the judge.

"Go ahead, Mr. Russell."

"I haven't lodged a complaint against Ms. Biekman – at my age, I'm not supposed to be capable of lodging one, or even understanding the charges. My parents haven't lodged a complaint. The source of the anonymous tip – whoever he or she might be – could have no possible basis for an accusation other than that we entered Ms. Biekman's dorm at the same time. I often get threatening texts or emails from people who think I'm some sort of prophet, or pretending to be, and I assume the complainant is one of these. He or she could have no idea what we were doing after we entered the dorm."

"Are you saying that nothing happened?"

"Yes."

"No further questions," said Berenson.

Barnes jumped on this in his redirect. "Are you saying – under oath – that you and Ms. Biekman never had sex together."

"That's what I'm saying," said Seth.

"Then what were you doing naked in the same bed?"

"Discussing Gandhi."

"What?" Barnes had no idea what Seth was talking about.

"Mahatma Gandhi, the freedom fighter who was considered a saint by the masses in India, often slept in the same bed with a beautiful naked woman to test his ability to resist temptation."

"Oh, for Christ's sake."

"Language, Counselor," said Landau.

Seth went on. "The whole point of the exercise was to practice *brahmacharya*, the Hindu ideal of sexual self control, more specifically, sexual abstinence. That's what we were doing naked in Ms. Biekman's bed."

Barnes couldn't have been more disgusted by Seth's excuse but he couldn't see a way around it and didn't want to pursue it until his summation. "No further questions."

In his summation, Barnes kept referring to Seth as "the victim." The jury didn't buy it, nor did anyone else in the courtroom.

31

Before he left for New Guinea, Seth spent one final night with Marike.

They made love, noting that Gandhi would be very disappointed.

"Did I ever thank you for lying on the stand?" said Marike.

"You just did."

"I never thought you could lie like that, with a straight face."

"One should never smirk while lying," said Seth.

Marike was still conflicted about Seth's many lives – it was just too far-fetched – and it was always possible that everything he said in the courtroom was true. But if he really was four hundred years old, wouldn't that somehow require him to be truthful? Wouldn't you learn honesty after four hundred years?

"Honesty can get you burned at the stake," said Seth. "Or locked up in a nuthouse. Honesty can destroy a marriage, ruin a relationship, get you fired from your job, make people who like you hate you. Not to mention, it would have destroyed your life. If I hadn't lied in the courtroom, you'd be in jail. No, there are much more important things than honesty."

"What about trust?" asked Marike. "Can you trust a person who lies?"

"That depends on why they lie and what they lie about." Seth put his arm around her and hugged her to him. "Is that you wanted to do on my last night in town, discuss morality?"

Marike laughed. "I don't want to discuss anything," she said, rolling over on top of him.

The next evening, Professor Olmsted accompanied Seth to Logan Airport in Boston and had a few minutes to talk before the security check.

"So if it turns out this sorceress is not what you think she is, you'll be back?" asked Olmsted.

"On the next flight."

"I know I'll lose a valuable resource, but it'd be thrilling if she's the one."

"If she is, I'll bring her back with me," said Seth. "If she'll come."

"If she's the high priestess of something, it may not be so easy."

"She also might be dead," said Seth. "Her letter was written six years ago. I've sent her a letter telling her I was coming but who knows if she'll get it, or even if I'll find the place."

A voice over the loudspeaker announced that the flight to Hong Kong, the first leg of his flight to Port Moresby, would be ready to board in 20 minutes and all passengers should be at the security checkpoint.

"I wonder what she'll be like?" asked Olmsted.

"A darker version of Ursula Andress in *She.*"

"I don't think I've seen that one."

"A beautiful goddess, ageless, sexy, cruel, who speaks in mysterious undertones, wears Egyptian headdresses and goes into trances, accompanied by beautiful naked acolytes to do her bidding and trap unwary explorers."

"Sounds like King Kong will show up at any moment," said Olmsted.

"On the other hand, she might *look* like King Kong," said Seth.

Olmsted laughed and Seth turned to go on the security line. "Goodbye, Professor. Hopefully, I'll see you again."

"If not …"

"If not I'll remember you for many lives to come."

32

The Cathy Pacific flight took over 15 hours. That was the easy part of the trip, in relative comfort, with excellent food and charming stewardesses especially attentive to a juvenile traveling alone.

Somewhere mid-flight, he lost interest in the movie and as he sat back to sleep, the memory of an old life entered his consciousness. This one was far, far back, at first merely a shard of a memory, a feeling of drunken despair, and then she remembered that she had been a woman with a terrible secret, a secret that had destroyed her. She was the lesser Lais of the Temple of Aphrodite in Corinth, not the famous Sicilian Lais who had her pick of the worshippers, not the rich Lais who turned down the wealthy Demosthenes for the unruly Diogenes (so poor he lived in a wine barrel), not the beautiful Lais who gave her wealth to adorn the temple. She had been lesser in beauty, wealth, charm, accomplishment and allure and in her devotion to the goddess, Aphrodite.

Like the greater Lais, she had been trained as a hetaera, she could converse on the topics of the day, she could dance to excite worshippers and play the flute to charm them. As a young girl, men would pay a mina for her talents.

Now, she would be content with an obul, which would go immediately for wine, the cheapest Naxos residue, worth drinking only for the effect. She drank it undiluted, which was said to promote insanity.

When her father sold her to the temple, he had envisioned a bright future for his whole family as Lais would amass enough wealth to support them in their old age. But he died young and her secret made her hideous in the eyes of Aphrodite.

Her worshippers fell to zero, she begged off other hetaera, her body disintegrated, she ate only the scraps nobody could digest, the garbage, she shook and sweated, she shrank to nothing and when she could no longer stand upright, all that was left was prayer. And when she prayed, her secret was out in the open. *For she prayed not to Aphrodite but to Artemis,* Artemis the chaste huntress. She had always prayed to Artemis. And Aphrodite had her revenge.

She remembered dissolving in misery, not in the temple itself but in a nook between stones halfway down the Akrokorinthus, the monolithic rock leading up to the temple. She called for water, she even called for wine. She didn't know if the passersby, men from the port of Corinth who came for the hetaera, were real or imaginary, for she also called to shadows, demons, men with fox heads and ram horns. No one responded.

The descent into Hong Kong brought Seth back to the present. The memory of his life as Lais left him shaken. He recalled another life that ended in an alcoholic haze, in Holland in the 1600's, but that of Lais was worse. She only lived to be twenty-five.

It was comforting to be in Chek Lap Kok airport in Hong Kong while waiting for his next flight. He could read the signs in Chinese and speak with some of the shopkeepers, most of whom spoke Mandarin as well as Cantonese, the prevalent language in Hong Kong, which Seth didn't speak. Even the people who spoke Mandarin had trouble understanding Seth, as he spoke the Wuhan dialect, which has its own pronunciation.

He had a few hours to kill and treated himself to goose and xiao long bao dumplings at a fancy restaurant in the West Hall. Although many Western travelers to Hong Kong spoke Chinese, a 15-year-old white boy speaking it, and with a regional accent, was a novelty to the waiters and they took pains to engage him in conversation.

He was hoping to get an Air Niugini flight nonstop to Port Moresby, Papua New Guinea, that took only 6 hours and 45 minutes, but it wasn't available. "Who would have thought that many people wanted to get to Port Moresby?" he thought. The only flight available was an Air Niugini Fokker 70 that once belonged to KLM, which flew first over Indonesia, thousands of miles out of the way, and stopped off at Brisbane, Australia, before continuing to Port Moresby.

By the time he reached Port Moresby, he was exhausted. Fortunately, there was a hotel at the airport where he could rest up for his 8:05 AM flight to Vanimo, without experiencing Port Moresby itself. As a 15-year-old, he would have been a mark for every criminal on the street so it was safer to avoid the city altogether. He didn't want anything to interrupt his quest.

He was back at the airport for his 8:05 AM flight to Vanimo, a Dash 8-400 Turboprop that stopped at Wewak and arrived at Vanimo at 11:10.

At the airport, Seth was told he should have stayed in Wewak because there were no flights to Telefomin from Vanimo. But he could hire a missionary plane from Wewok, which would take him to the interior.

Vanimo was a small town on the north coast, close to the border with Indonesian New Guinea. It was known as a surfer's paradise for its warm temperatures year round and a costal configuration that seemed to produce "the perfect wave" almost every time. Seth stayed at a hotel on the beach that looked like it had never been cleaned while he waited for a plane back to Wewak.

The next day, he returned to Wewak only to be told there was no regular plane service to Telefomin. But he could charter a plane from a Christian organization called Mission Aviation Fellowship, or MAF.

"Why didn't you hire a plane in Vanimo?" said a man who seemed to belong to the airport. "You didn't need to come here."

It turned out, a family of five had chartered a plane to return to Telefomin. "They're in Port Moresby at the moment, but they should be here sometime today."

The next day, with a family who spoke only Tok Pisan, a creole language that Seth didn't understand but could catch fragments of meaning from its English origins, he boarded a single engine 9-passenger Cessna Caravan for Telefomin. The pilot, a fresh-faced missionary, was surprised to see an American boy on his own. "Is someone meeting you in Telefomin?"

"I hope so," said Seth, who was beginning to regret coming at all.

"Not much to do there," said the pilot.

"I'm going to a village called Mindanna."

"Never heard of it. But as long as you're being met ..."

In less than three hours, they landed at a grass airstrip that was on the edge of a broad river leading through jungle. On the other side was a sprinkling of low buildings that might be considered a town. There was cargo on one side of the strip, a few trailer-like buildings and the MAF building, which was basically a wooden ranch house on stilts. The plane taxied to the MAF building where everyone got off. The family of five was met by animated relatives but there was no one for Seth.

A few boys came up to him and, in broken English, offered to be his guide to wherever he wanted to go.

"Shrunken head ceremony?" said one. "I show you."

Seth refrained from saying, 'I've already been a shrunken head,' but thought better of it. "No, thanks."

In the MAF building, he approached a man who seemed to be an airline official. "Excuse me, could you tell me how I'd get to Mindanna?"

"Mindanna? I don't know it."

"It's an Oksapmin village," said Seth.

"Oh yes, there's plane service to Oksapmin now. But I think the plane is out of service."

"Just my luck."

"But you can hire a guide to take you there. Very cheap." He pointed out the boy who had offered to show him the shrunken head ceremony.

33

It was not pleasant to be in a forest again. It brought back so many unpleasant memories of his life as a Shuar in the Amazon, as a pygmy in Bandiagara, as a San in Botswana. But more than that, there was the fear that he might end up here in his next life.

The boy took Seth's backpack, which was small, light and not overly filled, and they walked up a dirt road along the Sepik River. Old, broken down trucks passed them and a bus that seemed on its last legs rumbled by. When Seth inquired why they couldn't take a bus to Oksapmin, the boy had no answer, he didn't seem to understand the question.

His guide was perhaps twelve or thirteen years old, dressed in cutoffs, sneakers and an oversized Rangers T-shirt. His brown hair was cut short, slightly more than shaved, his skin was a child's skin, smooth and shiny, and his nose seemed too wide for his face. The boy, whose name was Itul, had obviously been instructed to make money guiding tourists but he evinced no interest in Seth whatsoever, where he came from, what he was doing there, although perhaps it was etiquette rather than lack of curiosity, or difficulty with the language.

After a few miles, they took a turn into a path that took them into the mountainous highlands. For a while they continued upwards through dense vegetation until they emerged into a path that seemed more of a ledge, which required intense concentration to avoid falling off. Seth was breathing hard and sweating profusely after only a short time; Itul, who was carrying Seth's backpack, would occasionally slow down to let Seth catch up to him. In other lives, the trek would have given him no trouble whatsoever, Seth thought. But in this one, he only had the body of a spoiled Westerner.

"Have you heard of a woman called Ybunlis?" asked Seth, during a quick break. "She's a priestess."

"A sorceress?" asked Itul.

"I don't know."

"They burn sorcerers," he said seriously.

I know only too well, thought Seth. "Have they burned any recently?"

"Last year, at Mount Hagen. A sorceress."

At another break, at the end of another long ledge, in a small clearing, Seth took his backpack, opened it and took out two granola bars. He offered one to Itul, who refused.

"How much further?" asked Seth.

"Not far. Three or four hours if it doesn't rain."

Just as night was falling, an exhausted Seth and a fresh Itul arrived at Oksapmin, which was basically a general store, a small school, an even smaller church and a building which was probably a government office of some kind. All were closed. There were no people anywhere. A short distance away was a scattering of ranch houses on stilts along an unpaved street.

"This is Oksapmin," said Itul.

"I expected something smaller," said Seth. Itul didn't get the joke.

Seth sat on the steps of the church to catch his breath while Itul tried the door. It was open and Itul looked inside for a moment to make sure it was empty of people and animals. "We spend the night here," he said. "Too many bugs outside."

It was a long time before Seth could get to sleep, lying on a hard wooden floor, which was nonetheless softer than a pew. For one, it was really too early to go to sleep. For another, he hadn't eaten anything other than a granola bar the entire day and he was feeling the pangs of hunger. But the principle thought that kept him awake was what awaited him tomorrow. Was this whole trip a bad idea? Was Ybunlis the real thing or just a smart woman who had convinced herself that she was reincarnated? Had he ended up in the middle of nowhere based on a whim?

He was more committed to this adventure than he wanted to be. And it was not something he could easily undo. He had an urge to walk back to Telefomin, hire a charter to Wewok or Vanimo, fly back to Port Moresby and then back to Boston, just to be in the comforting arms of civilization.

But he needed Itul to get back. He could never navigate those ledges on his own. Having many lives did not make him more courageous or more surefooted. It merely gave him perspective. He had no fear of death – that was temporary – but a fear of dying, of the pain, the discomfort, falling off a ledge and waiting at the bottom, broken and in agony.

But another fear crept in: what if in his next life, he ended up *here*, in this primitive country, where they burned witches, where there were over 800 languages, where a culture of poverty, superstition and revenge made living dangerous, and the only civilizing influence was a patronizing and demoralizing Christianity? Was there any way he could avoid this?

Would he ever be released from the whim of destiny? What was the point of countless lives if they didn't increase his power, his self-control, his mastery of some discipline …

Well, perhaps there were some positives. He increased in wisdom – slightly – in accumulated knowledge, in appreciation of the world's almost universal stupidity, and of the exceptions – the kind, intelligent, giving minority that almost made it worthwhile to exist.

Morning came and Seth and Itul waited for the general store to open. A family of four was also waiting outside. "Ask them if they know the way to Mindanna." said Seth.

Itul approached the father and spoke to him in Tok Pisin. They were in luck. The father clearly knew the route and pointed to a dense clump of jungle that seemed to have no openings whatsoever. He spoke for some time, heatedly.

Itul returned. "He says over there, follow the path to the place where the tree kangaroos fought in olden times, past the waterfall where the giant taipan lurks, past the God-Tree, over the Ok-bridge and then a mile to the clearing."

"Those were his words?" asked Seth.

"Pretty much."

"Did you understand any of what he was talking about, tree kangaroos and God-trees?" asked Seth.

"No," said Itul. "But here is where I leave you."

"Here?"

"I only agreed to take you to Oksapmin," said Itul. "I don't know the way from here."

"I'll find it."

They waited until the store opened and bought enough food for the rest of the day. Seth and Itul shared some sweet potato, kangkong greens and pork that had been cooked two days before, stocked up on chocolate bars and coke and food that was easy to carry.

When it was time to go their separate ways, Itul asked if Seth wanted a guide for the way back.

"Meet me here in two days," said Seth.

"You pay first."

Seth gave him the return fare, said goodbye, and headed for the wall of forest where the new path was supposed to begin.

For someone who had lived five lives in a jungle, it was not difficult to find the spot where the path began, a broken twig was a clear signal to enter an impenetrable thicket.

Seth plunged into the jungle and found that he had not been mistaken about the path. Most of the time, it was easy to follow and the insects were not as bad as they could be.

There was no way he could tell where the tree kangaroos fought in olden times, but he did come to a waterfall where a giant taipan was supposed to lurk. He knew that taipans were among the most venomous snakes in the world and could reach eight feet in length and he was hoping a giant one wouldn't come after him. Fortunately, nothing happened as he trekked past the waterfall.

He was curious about the "God-tree" that was supposed to be his next milestone. He had no idea what to look for; he envisioned a mighty banyan that covered an acre in roots and offshoots. But he saw nothing on that order. He passed a few gnarled specimens that might have qualified but at length he came upon a truly extraordinary tree. Its base was a tangle of giant roots massing around a thick trunk which was striped with red, yellow, blue, green and purple bark up the entire length of the tree and over its many trunks curving out from the main body. At the top were long thin red, orange and green leaves with red brushes and white puffs dangling from stems high above the forest canopy, barely visible to Seth's eye. He could imagine how many insects, birds and mammals lived in the precincts of the God-tree.

As he left the tree and continued on the path, he saw a man coming towards him wearing nothing but ragged shorts, carrying what looked like a musical instrument on his back. As he approached, Seth saw that his face and body had the complexion of mud, as if he had been rolling in it for days. Still, his expression was pleasant and he seemed not threatening.

Seth smiled at him and pointed to the path ahead of him. "Mindanna?" he said.

The man returned his smile, nodded and repeated, "Mindanna."

Seth went on and the path rose steadily, growing steeper and steeper until there could be no question that he was climbing rather than walking. The foliage on both sides hid the extent of steepness ahead and he had to stop several times to catch his breath.

When at last the path straightened out, he found himself on the edge of a chasm. A rickety rope bridge spanned the chasm and Seth hesitated a moment before setting foot on it. It was truly dangerous. The bridge literally swayed in the wind. Seth held on to the hand ropes on both sides and found himself sinking with each step. Still he managed to make his way about halfway across and then stopped.

On the other side, blocking the last four or five feet of the bridge, was a truly fearsome animal, a crocodile monitor, the largest lizard in the world after the Komodo dragon and the longest, sometimes reaching 10 feet. Its bite was known to be venomous and its temperament aggressive. Seth had read about it on the plane from Boston. It was not only ferocious but nimble; it spent much of its time in trees and it could leap from tree to tree. Presumably, it could scamper along the rope bridge faster than Seth could turn around and flee.

Since there was nothing else to do, Seth did nothing. He sat down on the bridge and waited. He looked at the lizard's round green snout with its pink forked tongue flicking in and out and its large curved claws on either side of its head. He saw its red eyes staring at him and stared back. How absurd to end his life in the mouth of a lizard, he thought. But he knew that animals rarely attack humans unless provoked. He supposed it depended how hungry the lizard was.

The two stared at one another for what seemed like hours but was probably less than twenty minutes. Then the lizard shuddered, backed off the bridge awkwardly and moved off into the bush. Perhaps it got bored, he thought.

Seth waited another five minutes, then cautiously continued his way over the bridge and onto the path on the other side of the chasm, hyper alert for signs of the lizard.

After another mile of relatively easy walking, Seth heard voices in the distance, women chattering, the screams and laughter of children. Soon he came to a clearing where women were preparing food, children were running wild and farther away, men were carving, mending or just smoking. The open area was surrounded on three sides by thatched huts, raised on stilts, with roofs that sloped upwards. In the center of the area was a large fire where food was cooking. It was a familiar scene. He could have been among the Shuar, in Botswana, in Bandiagara, in any primitive society. Just a few details changed.

They were all short, larger than pygmies but shorter than Western adults. Most of the women wore grass skirts and nothing on top. The children were naked. The men wore shorts, although two were naked and one wore a penal sheath. All of the adults wore necklaces of shells, beads and bone. As this was not a festival day, none wore the spectacular face paint and elaborate costumes Seth had seen in the guide books or on the stamps. Most of the men had the slim, muscular bodies of hunters and warriors but the women, even the younger ones, seemed dried out, their breasts hung down as if they had been drained of milk and were now useless flaps against their bodies.

As in all of these tribes, his entrance caused a sensation. Everyone gathered around him, feeling his clothes, touching his limbs, laughing at his general appearance. When a man came up to him, he asked, "Mindanna?"

The man nodded to confirm the village and then spoke to several other men in a language that was not Tok Pisan or any language that Seth had ever heard. Since Papua New Guinea has over 800 languages, this was not surprising.

"Ybunlis?" said Seth.

He had to repeat the name several times before he was understood. The name evoked chatter and laughter, probably at his accent but also at the sound of a familiar name from a white stranger. Seth put his hand over his forehead and pretended to search while he repeated the name.

There was much chatter and laughter at this but eventually an older man wearing ragged shorts and a necklace made from bone approached him with a serious expression and beckoned to follow him. "Ybunlis," he said, which sounded totally different from Seth's pronunciation.

Seth followed him and was in turn followed by what seemed like half the village. They passed through the ring of thatched huts to a slightly larger hut at a short distance from the ring. There was nothing to distinguish this hut from any other except a wider frame. It was also on stilts.

The man gestured at Seth to wait while he called inside. Getting no response, he climbed the step ladder leading to the front entrance and called again. Perhaps the person inside responded but Seth didn't hear it. The man went inside and Seth could hear something of a conversation, although it was hard to concentrate as a group of women and children were still pulling at his clothing and touching his skin.

Despite the distraction, Seth felt a growing excitement that perhaps his quest had come to an end. Perhaps there was someone in the world like him. On the other hand, why couldn't this Ybunlis be faking, like all the others? He tried to hold his emotions in abeyance while he waited.

Inside, in a dimly lit room, a conversation was taking place in Oksapmin, the language of Mindanna and the surrounding villages.

"Mother," said the man. "He's here."

A woman responded. "Is this the foreigner who waited for the lizard at the bridge?"

The man said it was.

"Is he from the government?"

"I don't think so," said the man.

"Is he another anthropologist, come about our counting system?" (The Oksapmin had a unique counting system where the numbers corresponded to parts of the body in a particular order and reached up to 27.)

"I don't think so," said the man. "He asked for you by name."

"How old is he?"

"Not fully grown," said the man.

The woman paused for a moment. "Show him in, then leave us alone."

At length the man reappeared and beckoned Seth to climb the ladder and go inside.

34

The hut was dark. Seth expected to see a fairly bare interior, a few cooking or eating implements and a straw mat, but as his eyes adjusted to the light, he was surprised to see a table and chairs, a primitive fireplace and, most astonishing of all, a wall of books in various languages. There were books and newspapers on the table and strewn throughout the hut. A section of one wall was for kitchen and eating utensils and, in the middle of the room, was a low desk, stocked with pens and paper.

Behind the desk, sitting in a chair and, given the dim light, almost invisible at first glance, was a wizened old woman, who seemed to blend in with the dark. Only her eyes, which were strikingly green, stood out in the light. In a strong voice, she asked Seth a question in a language he didn't understand.

His heart sank. Perhaps she was just a village elder after all. But who had written the letter? "Do you speak English?" Seth asked.

"Aah," she sighed, flashing a charming smile. When she spoke, it was in an upper class English accent. "I haven't heard English in a long time. Come closer. My eyes are old."

"Your English is perfect."

"Please sit down," said the woman. "You must be tired."

"You are Ybunlis?"

"Yes."

"It hasn't been easy to reach you."

"And who are you?" asked Ybunlis. "I sent out a great many letters without knowing if anyone received them or, indeed, if any of the recipients are still alive."

"You sent your letter when I was nine and now I'm fifteen. My name is Seth Russell."

"And why did I write you?"

"You wrote me that you'd heard about a song I sang in an extinct language."

"What language?"

"Kemi, one of the languages of the Sami people of northern Scandinavia."

"Hm," she commented. She clearly didn't remember the details of her letter. "My sons sometimes go into Oksapmin for supplies. There's a post office there and they can mail my letters and pick up mail and newspapers. That's probably where I heard about your song."

"You wrote me that we might have something in common."

"Come closer," she said. "Is this possible?"

"You said you knew Etruscan."

Ybunlis nodded and tested Seth on his knowledge of languages. She spoke to him in Chinese; he answered in the dialect of Wuhan, which is difficult for a Mandarin speaker to understand.

She spoke in modern Arabic; Seth answered in medieval Arabic.

"Before Arabia, I spoke Swedish," said Ybunlis. Seth answered in 15th Century Swedish. "Yes, I understand your Swedish but it's changed much since I last spoke it."

Ybunlis tried a few other languages that Seth didn't understand. Then she spoke in a language he knew well. "I don't suppose you speak Nharo."

"I can't believe this!" said Seth. "Yes, I speak Nharo."

In Nharo, she said, "It sounds like we lived there around the same time. I was Tshebe-ki-sa ..."

Seth responded in Nharo. "... of Nwaxe? I was the grandfather of your joking cousin."

"You knew Gwa'nae?"

"She fed me when I could no longer walk."

"This is amazing." She was clearly as excited as he was. She tried the Seminole dialect of Muscogee, and then Tibetan, neither of which Seth knew. He tried Heian Japanese, which she didn't recognize.

She tried ancient Greek. "Where were you in the time of Demosthenes, when Brasidas captured Amphipolis?"

"I was Lais of Corinth," said Seth.

"The temple priestess?"

"Not the famous one."

Ybunlis laughed. "No, the other one who drank herself to death."

They both leaned back and smiled, clearly amazed to have found one another. For a few moments, they couldn't speak at all, only smile. Finally, Ybunlis said, "We've been looking for each other for a long time."

"I wondered if there was anyone else like me, even before Greece."

"I sent letters to everyone who seemed possible. You're the first to respond."

"Have you seen any patterns?" asked Seth.

"No," said Ybunlis, "I've looked for them but what we become seems entirely random."

"But always on this earth. And always human."

"So it would seem."

"By the way, your English accent …"

Ybunlis saluted. "Captain Addison Hodges, 1ˢᵗ Battalion, Grenadier Guards, killed at Ypres in World War 1."

Seth countered that he'd been a *centurion primus pilus* in the Roman army of Agrippa, killed at Actium.

Now that they had tested one another and both were certain that the other was legitimate, they relaxed into a more normal conversation. They had both searched for ways to exert some influence over their fate but had come up empty. In some of the Buddhist traditions, there is a 49-day period between incarnations in which one's karmic propensities, or your own enlightened will, can choose your next birth. But neither of them had experienced an in-between state. They died and woke up as something else, beginning with a *tabula rasa* until their memories from other lives emerged.

In many ways, they were more fortunate than their short-lived counterparts. By far the most important way was that they no longer feared extinction. It was possible that normal humans had multiple lives but not remembering them made each life a separate extinction. For all practical purposes, normal humans had a single life, which ended at death.

But for Seth and Ybunlis, immortality had extraordinary consequences. They no longer had any interest in religion, for example. They'd been raised in too many of them and they didn't see that one was better than another. Monotheism seemed to have produced particularly brutal religions, but then polytheism seemed absurd, although Seth still had a fondness for Artemis, which amused Ybunlis.

Likewise, all nations seemed equally good and bad – the same country could produce a Bach and a Hitler – but nationalism seemed as absurd as polytheism. That Americans or the English could consider themselves superior to Rwandans or Papua New Guineans was an evil in itself. *America First* or *Rule Britannia* or *Deutchland Uber Alles* seemed mind-bogglingly stupid.

They had both been black, white and yellow, male and female, rich and poor (although neither had been royalty) so they could dispense with racism, sexism and aristocratic disdain or proletarian resentment.

They no longer felt envy, outrage, greed, a host of emotions that required only a few lives to dispense with entirely. Glory and honor seemed particularly pernicious, as were all the militaristic virtues.

What was left? They still felt fear, mostly of the process of dying or being killed. Seth still felt the flames of the stake. They both felt astonishment at the state of the world. They both could give and accept love and desire. They both felt sadness at watching their loved ones grow old and die, at leaving them behind. They both mourned the loss of cherished friends and mentors.

Ybunlis wondered if there were more immortals like them.

"I wonder as well," said Seth. "But we can *make* some more."

"As you can see, I'm past child-bearing age," said Ybunlis.

"In *this* life," said Seth.

Ybunlis nodded abstractedly and switched the subject to dinner. "Let me make you some dinner. You must be starving."

Ybunlis rose and went outside to give instructions to her son, who had been waiting nearby the entire time. Soon a group of women arrived with a pot of *mumu*, pork and sweet potatoes stewed with coconut cream, and plates of dumplings made of sago and bananas. Ybunlis brought out an herb from her hut and mixed it into the stew, and then crushed another batch in her hand and sprinkled it over the dumplings.

"This is delicious," said Seth, ladling stew into a small bowl and eating it with his fingers. The dumplings were wrapped in banana leaves.

"It's a holiday meal, for special occasions," said Ybunlis.

"There's a flavoring I don't recognize," said Seth.

"It's an herb that grows wild in this area. I've never come across it anywhere else."

"A type of nigella?" Seth speculated.

As they ate, they reminisced about the food they had eaten over the centuries. "China was the best," said Ybunlis.

"No, France," said Seth.

"I've never been there."

"We ate grasshoppers in the Amazon," said Seth.

"Maggots in Greenland."

"Bat paste."

"Cod sperm."

"It's a good thing we had seven years to get used to these foods," said Ybunlis.

They continued eating their meal in a bemused silence.

"Now to business," said Ybunlis. "If we both die now, we'll be the same child-bearing age in the next life. The problem will be, how to find each other."

"That's not the only problem," said Seth. "We don't know *when* we'll reincarnate. Or what we'll reincarnate as – we might both be the same sex and not be able to reproduce. We might end up in different decades or centuries."

"We have to assume around the same time. But we have to allow for some variations ... not decades ..."

"I suggest we wait till we're 25," said Seth, "when we have enough independence to go where we like."

"Unless one of us ends up in a place we can't leave."

"Well, that's certainly possible," said Seth. "To be a woman in much of the world means we're trapped. When I was the fourth wife of Sheik Abdrashid Yusuf Ahmen in Somalia, I was essentially a slave, used for sex and household chores. There was no way out."

"As I was in China," said Ybunlis. "a slave to the Number One wife. Hopefully, things have changed but we can never be sure."

They debated when and where to meet and finally agreed on Westminster Abbey in London, near the tomb of Chaucer in the Poet's

Corner at 12 noon on April 25, 2045, 25 years hence. They discussed alternative dates and places, aware that so much could go wrong.

"*When* should we do it?" said Seth.

"No sense putting it off. I'd like to say goodbye to my children and grandchildren and two great grandchildren. Do you have relatives?"

"I called them before I left, told them I might not be back."

"That's always the sad part," said Ybunlis. "I've never gotten used to it."

"*How* shall we do it?" asked Seth.

"That's already been taken care of."

"The herb," said Seth, looking at his food.

"When you go to sleep tonight, you'll wake up in another life," said Ybunlis.

They finished what would be their last meal in silence. Evidently, the effects of the herb wouldn't be noticeable for several hours.

"Y'know," Ybunlis mused, "sometimes I think about all my mothers as a single mother, as if they've all merged."

"Only the good mothers," said Seth. "The bad ones stand out."

"I don't think I've ever had a mother who didn't love me."

"Sometimes it didn't seem like love."

"True."

With Seth's help, Ybunlis rose from where they were sitting and beckoned to her son to help her walk. "Well, I suppose I better prepare my clan for two dead bodies."

"What will they do with us?" asked Seth.

"In Tibet, they left our carcasses out for the vultures and ground our bones into dust. Here they're not so civilized."

25 YEARS LATER

35

At noon, April 25, 2045, Westminster Abbey was packed with tourists. They tried to limit access to a smaller number but so many tourists stayed longer than expected that there was quite a traffic jam inside the Abbey and a long queue outside.

As the burial ground of kings from Edward the Confessor on up and the final resting place of the flower of British civilization, it was a place for lingering and contemplation, if only the tourists wouldn't get in the way.

The Poet's Corner, in the South Transept, was one of the *must* attractions, filled with statues and plaques for luminaries like Milton and Dickens. The first tomb, placed there in 1400, was that of Geoffrey Chaucer. In 1556, his remains were transferred to a more elaborate tomb of gray marble with the inscription, in Latin, that spoke of the greatness of Chaucer, "the bard who struck the noblest strains."

Wriggling his way through the tourists on the way to the Poet's Corner, past a man with his wife in full burqa, past several worshipful parents and their disinterested children, was a large, muscular man with a gold-red beard and curly red hair. He could be Irish or Russian or Scandinavian, a Viking perhaps, or a Celtic warrior. He wore jeans and a blue dress shirt, with the sleeves rolled up.

He had to wait for a few minutes while a guide explained something to his tour group in German. When they left, he was able to stand directly in front of the tomb and examine the inscription more closely.

He checked his watch and went back to examining the tomb when he became aware of a large presence behind him. He turned around and saw an impossibly tall woman smiling at him. She was at least 6 foot 5, perhaps larger, but elegant and beautiful, with a face that seemed a mixture of Indian and Chinese. She was wearing a dress of green silk and looked vibrantly healthy.

"Ybunlis?" said the woman.

"Seth?" said the man, incredulously.

"I came a little early, so I looked around a bit."

The man extended his hand. 'You've grown."

The tall woman took it. "Khin Khin Aung, from Myanmar."

"Davin O'Shaughnessey, from Ireland."

They looked at each other and smiled. "This worked out perfectly," said Khin Khin."

"So it would seem. We're both around the same age, one of us is a man, one of us is a woman, and both of us seem healthy, hopefully fertile. So far so good."

"In case you're wondering, yes, I'm a basketball player, on Myanmar's national team."

"So our children will be both immortal and tall."

They left the Poet's Corner and walked back towards the main entrance. The crowd of tourists, headed for the Poet's Corner, parted quickly to let them through, perhaps intimidated by Khin Khin's size.

As they walked, Seth (now Khin Khin) put her arm around Davin's (Ybunlis') shoulder.

"I feel like we're like Adam and Eve," said Davin.

"Let's hope so."

The End